YOUNG LOVE

STELLA MACLEAN

Young Love
Stella MacLean
Copyright 2021 Ruth MacLean

Cataloguing and Publication information is available from The Canadian ISBN Service System, Library and Archives Canada.

Title: Young Love/Stella MacLean

Identifiers:

ISBN: Print 978-1-7778199-0-3| EPUB 978-1-7778199-1-0

Formatting Services: Sweet' N Spicy Designs
Cover Design: Elizabeth Turner Stokes

First Love:
that life-stopping moment that changes everything...

CHAPTER ONE

1976

Sarah Maddison breathed in the glorious scent of freshly cut lilacs—armloads of them in the corner of the gymnasium. Tiny lights glittered along the edge of the stage, over the doors and windows, and the basketball hoops were draped with purple and yellow bunting, Frampton High School's colors.

She'd been given the job of decorating for the prom, and she couldn't be more pleased with her efforts. She loved to create beautiful spaces, to pick the colors for rooms, to design happy places for people to live their lives. And she couldn't believe that she'd been accepted to go to Hastings College in the fall to study interior design. So many things were so perfect in her life; every day was better than the last.

Sarah smiled in contentment as she and Kevan placed the stubby candles nestled in glass pots on each of the white clad tables that ringed the large area. Kevan McElroy hadn't left her side all day, and she basked in the idea that he was now truly hers.

"Whew! That's it, I guess. I'm glad to be finished, aren't you?" she asked, not the least bit glad. She'd cherished every moment she spent with Kevan.

"Don't wish your life away," Kevan teased, taking the last candles from her hands and placing them on a nearby table.

The sounds of the room faded as Kevan reached for her. "Every time I see that look in your eyes..." he murmured, pulling her behind a huge potted rubber tree to kiss her.

"Be careful," she whispered. Tingling heat charged down her spine. She wanted him to kiss her again, to claim her the way he had two nights ago.

"Or what?" Kevan eyed her, his cocky grin issuing a challenge as he nestled closer to her. She breathed in the scent of his cologne. His powerful hands slid down over her waist toward her bottom, his touch suggestive.

Her cheeks flamed, and she dropped her gaze, as she toyed with the locket around her neck. Crazy in love and under a moonlit night they'd gone all the way for the second time in the last two nights. The first time in the back of his car, he'd been loving and gentle, although she'd been terrified. It had hurt a little, but she'd never admit that to a living soul. It was what Kevan wanted and she'd wanted it, too. Everything would be all right. Kevan loved her.

Then last night it had been so different. They'd gone to a motel on the highway south of Boston, a place she'd never been. At first, she hadn't wanted to go into the room, her mother's admonishments about loose women, ringing in her ears. Once inside, with the door closed, she felt a little better. And when Kevan took her in his arms, every doubt vanished. He'd held her close, his arms tender, his voice soft against her ear as he told her again how much he loved her. When he undressed her, she had never felt more desirable, or so beautiful as when he lifted her onto the bed and lay down beside her.

This morning it was as if their life together had begun. When she'd gotten home last evening, she'd been excited and a little afraid that her parents might see in her face what she'd been doing. Instead, she'd been greeted with hugs and kisses and found out she'd been awarded the first full scholarship ever given to a woman at Hastings. Much to her embarrassment her parents had been on the phone all evening telling all their friends and relatives about their only child's plans for the future.

High-pitched laughter in one corner of the gymnasium invaded the private space between them, making Sarah self-conscious that someone might see them. What would her classmates say if they knew what she and Kevan had done?

She hated herself for worrying about what people thought. But she knew how much her classmates gossiped over girls who slept around. She'd also heard those girls brag about what they'd done, while she'd always harbored her mother's belief that it was wrong to have sex before marriage.

She and Kevan hadn't waited until they were married, but they were sure about their feelings.

He'd given her the beautiful locket as his commitment to their relationship. And last night he'd said that the locket would do until he could afford to give her an engagement ring.

After last night he'd been so attentive, so sweet. And even though he'd told her over and over how much he loved her, it still felt like a dream. "You didn't have to stay and help me with all this," she said, glancing around the huge space.

"Where else would I be?" he asked, a mock frown creasing the smoothness of his forehead.

All her doubts faded as she glanced up at him. "I wouldn't want to be anywhere else, either," she whispered, sliding her fingers along the cleft of his chin.

He raised her face to meet his gaze, his fingers feather-light against her skin. His hands swept up her back, toward the hook on her lace bra. "I will never forget last night," he said.

It all happened so fast, so unexpectedly, that they hadn't had a chance to think about birth control. "Last night—"

"Last night was everything I've ever wanted," Kevan murmured close to her ear, sending tendrils of need easing down her body.

"It was?" She touched the locket where it rested along the lacey edge of her bra. Forgetting all her mother's warnings about not leading a guy on, Sarah pressed her body to his.

"And we'll be careful, I promise. I went to the drugstore this morning."

"Oh, Kevan, maybe we should've waited. I *can't* get pregnant."

"Trust me. You won't."

"Are you sure?" she asked, wishing they were somewhere private.

"I am," he murmured, knitting his fingers into her hair.

"Well, you'd better keep your word." She gave him a playful shove as she smiled up into his gloriously blue eyes, fringed by dark eyelashes.

"They'll never be anyone for me but you." His thumb slipped under the gold chain that held the locket. "You'll always be a part of my life," he said, his voice a warm caress against her cheek.

"I love you," Sarah whispered.

"I love you, too. So much." He held her gently, his kiss whisking the air from her lungs.

In that one moment, Sarah realized she'd never love anyone the way she loved Kevan.

Abruptly his lips left hers. "Damn! I forgot. Dad wants me to meet him at the house around 6:00. He said it was urgent. I know we planned to go to Walden's Lodge for dinner before the dance, but I won't be able to make it. I'm sorry."

Disappointment clouded her happiness. She wanted to go with him to the restaurant, to be seen with the president of the senior class. She was so proud of him, of them. But there'd be other dinners at fine restaurants… "I guess it's all right. We could go to the lake and watch the moon rise after the dance."

"Making love in the moonlight is so much fun." He gave her a cheeky grin. "I'll get my penguin suit on and pick you up around 7:00."

"Better yet, why don't you meet me here? Emma Lawler is a little anxious about tonight. This is her first official event as head of the social committee."

"Sarah Maddison, lady with responsibilities, comes to the rescue one more time."

"You got it."

"See you later." He kissed her fingers before striding across the gymnasium floor and out the door.

CHAPTER TWO

Sarah fiddled with the beaded strap on her evening bag and glanced around at her classmates who stood in small groups, their voices tight with excitement. She let her fingers drift over the soft velvet folds of her skirt. Despite the small complication caused by Kevan's father, Sarah was sure tonight would be everything she could wish for. She pictured Kevan in his tuxedo, his arm circling her waist as he led her onto the dance floor. He was so handsome, and they had such plans for tonight after the prom. She would have him all to herself in the moonlight.

If he ever got there. Not wanting to appear anxious, she resisted the urge to let her gaze search the gymnasium one more time. *Where was Kevan?* The music would start any minute, and she wanted to dance the first waltz with him. Sarah loved the way Kevan danced so close she could feel the beating of his heart.

Feeling conspicuous, Sarah gave in to the urge and looked quickly around, hoping to see someone in the same predicament. Coming through the doors of the gymnasium was her best friend, Cindy Underhill. Relief whipping through her she hurried over to her friend.

Doug Cooper, a classmate, was walking beside Cindy, a goofy grin on his face, his hair slicked back. *Doug was Cindy's date for the senior prom?* Cindy, the single most beautiful girl in her graduating class, wouldn't be caught dead with someone like Doug. It didn't make sense. Doug was the last person in the whole of Frampton High that Cindy would date.

Cindy and her younger brother, Brad, were two of the most popular kids in the school, and Cindy could have any guy she wanted. Sarah had always been just a little bit envious of Cindy. Her parents had money; her dad worked as the head accountant at McElroy Manufacturing, and she could do pretty well as she pleased.

Cindy floated toward Sarah, the long taffeta folds of her emerald-green skirt undulating around her hips as she walked. Her gold-highlighted brown curls were held off her face with mother-of-pearl combs. A long strand of pearls stood out against her clear white skin, making her plunging neckline seem even more revealing. "Wow. What a dress."

"You like it?" Cindy twirled around, nearly bumping into Doug.

"You look absolutely gorgeous," Sarah said, giving Cindy a heart-felt hug of welcome.

"Thanks, I needed to hear that. I have something to prove tonight. And what about you? You look stunning in that dress. Blue velvet brings out the blonde highlights in your hair," Cindy said, returning the hug.

"I thought you were bringing Barry to the dance, not Doug." Sarah raised her eyebrows in question.

"Major fight. I'll explain later." Cindy glanced around. "Where's Kevan?"

"Some big discussion with his father couldn't wait."

"You're kidding. Tonight, of all nights his father has to have a meeting with him? That's strange."

"You're telling me. We were both looking forward to the first waltz and if he doesn't hurry up, we're going to miss it." Sarah searched the room again, looking for Kevan's familiar face.

"Looks like we both need a little consoling. Meet me at Bennie's for a soda tomorrow morning at ten and give me all the details, and I'll tell you what that snake-in-the-grass Barry did," Cindy said.

How could Cindy be so calm about Barry not being with her for her graduation prom? What was she going to do if Kevan didn't show up soon? Sarah nodded and forced a smile, her eyes searching the gymnasium impatiently.

"See you later then. I've got to go." Cindy took Doug's arm and headed to the dance floor.

The opening notes of Bobby Vinton's "Roses are Red" began. Longing slid through Sarah as she looked around one more time. Smiling graduates and their dates were moving onto the dance floor, leaving Sarah alone with her anxiety.

What could be keeping Kevan? He'd said he would be late, but this was ridiculous. *Should she try to call him?* There was a pay phone outside in the parking lot. She'd never called his house. In all the weeks they'd been together, there'd never been a reason. Kevan had always been so attentive.

Unable to wait any longer, Sarah skirted the tables and walked over to the entrance. The damp night air rushed toward her as she dashed down the steps. Somewhere out in the parking lot she heard a car door slam. Away from the muted light of the street lamps a man walked toward her, his loping stride so familiar.

"Kevan," she called out. Heedless of her billowing skirt and the hours she'd spent arranging her hair, Sarah ran to him.

She noticed his jeans and rumpled T-shirt first. The tense lines around his eyes were visible, even in the uncertain light of the parking lot. "Kevan, what is it?" she asked, holding out her arms.

He stopped just short of her reach. "Sarah," he said, his voice lacking its usual vigor, "there's a problem. I can't stay here with you."

"Why? What's wrong?" She reached for his hand.

The stiff set of his shoulders warned her off. His eyes were dark, his jaw clenched as he shook his head. "Don't, Sarah. I have to go away. Please don't."

Shock reverberated through her. This couldn't be happening. Kevan loved her.

Hot, sticky tears smudged her cheeks. "You were supposed to be here tonight. With me. This is *our* night, our time together. Tell me what's going on. I love you, Kevan. How could you leave me?"

Sarah swiped at her tears, fighting the urge to throw her arms around him. She had too much pride to force herself on Kevan, and he clearly didn't want to touch her. "Did something happen to your dad?"

"I can't talk right now." He rubbed his jaw, grimacing in pain.

"Kevan, are you hurt?"

His glance edged past her. "I'm fine."

"No. You're not." Sarah moved closer. "What's wrong with your cheek? Is that a bruise?"

"Sarah, never mind about my face." He began to reach for her, then stopped. "Please understand I don't have a choice. My father knows about us."

"He knows about us," she echoed. "What do you mean? Hasn't he known about us all along?"

Kevan rested his hands on his hips as his eyes studied the ground between them.

"You kept our relationship from your father?"

He nodded, but didn't raise his eyes. "I knew my father wouldn't approve."

"Kevan, look at me," she demanded.

He didn't meet her gaze.

"We're only weeks away from leaving for college, starting our life together. What has your father got to do with us? Why didn't you tell him about us before now?" She put out her hands but the flash of warning in his eyes forced them back to her sides.

"Sarah, I can't tell you very much, at least not yet. But things will get better soon. You have to trust me on this. You have to."

"I do trust you, but I don't understand why you can't tell me what's happened."

"My father wants me to go to Ireland," he said, "to the electronics plant there—"

"Ireland? Why Ireland?"

"He wants me to work for my Uncle Seamus. It won't be for long," he whispered his Adam's apple straining against his throat as his gaze searched hers.

"What about college? Will you be back in time for college this fall?"

"I'll be back with you as soon as I can…. It'll all be over in a little while, and we'll be together like we planned."

"But Kevan, why can't we be together now? Tonight?"

"Sarah, this is such a mess, but I'll explain it all once I figure out what to do. You have to believe in us," he whispered, his eyes dark with misery. "You have to."

"Oh, Kevan, I wanted tonight to be special." Needing to touch him, to feel his body next to hers, she moved closer.

His arms went around her. "I know you did. So did I. And I'll be back. Believe me." He held her close and the solid thud of his heart allowed her to hope that everything was still okay between them. She clung to him, to his strength, breathing in his scent. Surely this was some sort of mistake.

He smoothed her hair from her face. "Sarah, I'm flying out in a few hours."

Tears stung her eyes again. "I'll go with you. I don't care where we are as long as we're together."

"No. You can't come with me. But you'll wait for me?" he asked, his expression bleak.

"Always," she whispered, hugging him to her.

His sudden intake of breath and a muffled moan startled her. "Kevan, did I hurt you?"

He moved out of her embrace, his movement awkward and so unlike him. "I fell."

"When?"

"An hour or so ago. On the stairs. I hurt my ribs. It's not serious."

"Did you see a doctor?"

"Don't worry about it."

"Don't worry? You're injured; you're leaving, and I'm not supposed to worry?"

"Sarah, I have no choice but to be on that plane tonight...by myself."

Her heart beating erratically, Sarah made one last try to get him to tell her more. To explain why he had to go, what his father said. "Look at me."

Sarah saw the self-loathing in his eyes and her heart rose in agony. "Whatever is wrong, we can fix it, you and I," she said urgently. "We have our whole lives ahead of us. If your father wants you to go to Ireland for a while, I'll go with you. We can come back and go to college. You can't just walk away from me. We love each other. You'd never hurt me this way."

With a shuddering sigh, Kevan turned and started back toward his car.

Tossing her pride, Sarah raced after him. "You can't leave me like this! You can't! Why do you have to go?"

Kevan turned back to face her, anxiety clouding his once-adoring eyes. "I have no choice. I have to leave tonight."

"No!" Sarah wailed as she cast frantically about for some explanation. "Doesn't your father approve of me? How could he not like me when he hasn't even met me?"

"Sarah, please don't do this to yourself."

"*Do what?* Beg the man who loves me to stay with me?" Her

voice shook. She stared at him, waiting for any sign that he might retract his horrifying words.

The air around them stilled.

Was he dumping her because he'd gotten what he wanted from her? Was she just someone to toss aside after she'd had sex with him? After all, their families moved in different circles. His father, the manufacturing plant owner; hers, a laborer there. This wasn't the eighteenth century though... The world had changed. Standing there staring at him, hoping he'd relent and stay with her, she faced the reality his eyes had hinted at. "I'm not good enough for you, for your family. Is that it?"

"That's not true!" Kevan half-turned toward her.

"Then tell me the truth."

"I'll be back home from Ireland as soon as I can. That's all I can say for now."

Struggling to control the trembling in her hands, Sarah grabbed the gold chain around her neck and pulled on it. But it didn't break. "If I'm not good enough for your family why did you give me the locket?" she sobbed, tears running free down her cheeks as she yanked on it one more time. The chain broke in her hand, sending the locket skittering across the parking lot.

"No! I want you to keep that with you until I can come back."

"I don't care about the locket," she sobbed, her tears splashing down the front of her prom dress.

"Sarah, please don't cry. Please don't. I have to go. If I don't, someone might get hurt..." Kevan plowed his fingers through his hair, his gaze fixed on a point somewhere beyond her.

"What about *me*? What about how you're hurting me?"

He reached for her, then stopped, his hands suspended above her shoulders.

She held her breath, her whole body craving his touch.

His fingers hovered over her, then came to rest at his sides. "I made a promise. Sarah, please don't hate me."

"I could never hate you. Oh, Kevan, tell me what's going on. Whatever it is, we can work it out. That's what you always said… You and I, we can work anything out, because we love each other. Take me with you," she begged.

"I can't," he said, before turning away from her.

Shocked, struggling to find the right words, the words that would make Kevan come back to her, Sarah followed him to his car.

"Please. Don't leave me like this. What about our future together, our plans?" she coaxed him, her heart a dead weight in her chest.

With shoulders hunched, he kept on walking away from her.

She hesitated, words of need on her lips, her heart pounding with dread, as she watched him get into his car. Rooted to the spot she watched as he pulled out of the parking lot onto the street.

CHAPTER THREE

*F*eeling faint and with tears streaming down her face, Sarah leaned against the car parked next to where she was standing. Her mind reeled over what had just happened. She was still standing there when she heard Cindy call her name.

"I'm over here," she cried out, her voice shaking.

Cindy rushed up to her. "Where did you go? I've been looking all over for you. Doug is such an idiot! He has ruined the prom for me. After all the time and effort I put into getting ready…and this dress." She smoothed her hands over the taffeta folds of the skirt billowing about her hips. "I don't know what gets into me…or maybe they aren't really men yet," she said her gaze swinging in a wide arc covering the parking lot before returning to Sarah. Squinting in the pale light from the street lamp she asked. "Why are you out here alone? You've been crying. Oh, Sarah, what happened?"

"Kevan was here, but he had to leave. I…I don't get what's going on." Sarah wrapped her arms around her friend's neck and hugged her close. "He says he's leaving for Ireland tonight. He doesn't know when he'll be back."

"You got to be kidding! What is going on in this world? First Barry drops me and I'm stuck with Doug. Now Kevan acts like a jerk and leaves you waiting at the prom." She held Sarah by the shoulders looking into her eyes for a few seconds. "But I guess you're a lot worse off than I am. Tell you what. Why don't we go for a burger at the Buck-a-Burger? I've got Mom's car, and I can still drive," Cindy said, a wry tone in her voice.

"I don't... I want to go home," Sarah said, smudging her eye makeup with her fingers.

"No. You and I spent a lot of money and time looking like the divas we are, and our night is ruined. We are not going home. We are going to eat and trash the men in our lives." Cindy patted her on the back. "We girls got things to talk about. Let's go."

Numbly Sarah followed her to the car and climbed into the passenger seat, careful not to snag her dress in the door. Cindy drove out of the parking lot, accelerating as she reached the street. "This has not been a good night."

They reached the burger place, parked, and got out. Sarah didn't want to see anyone she knew. Trying to talk to Cindy was one thing. Trying to make conversation with anyone else was out of the question.

"It's a beautiful night so I think we should get our food and sit outside at the picnic tables. What do you say?" Cindy asked.

"Whatever..."

They went in, their billowing skirts swirling around them as they approached the order counter. The kid behind the counter let out a low, long whistle.

"Why are you staring at us?" Cindy demanded.

"I'm allowed to admire the clients that come to my order space," the young man said, unflapped by Cindy's attitude.

"Fine. While you're doing that, get us two burgers with the works, fries and root beer."

"Will do." The young man stared at Sarah, a look of adoration on his face. "You really look pretty."

"Come on, Sarah, let's find a place to sit," Cindy said, ignoring the young man. She led the way to a booth in the corner. "We'll wait here for our orders and then take them outside."

Once settled with their skirts tucked around their legs, Sarah looked at her friend and began to cry.

"Oh, Sarah, please don't cry. It can't be that bad," Cindy said, her voice soothing as she searched her evening bag for a tissue and passed it to Sarah.

"I'm sorry." Sarah sniffled, taking the tissue. "Kevan arrived, told me he was leaving for Ireland, and then left me standing in the parking lot." She went on to explain to Cindy what had happened. When she finished, Cindy's eyes were filled with tears. "Men can be such... I'm not supposed to swear. I've sworn off it actually." Cindy twirled her hair through her fingers. "What do you want to do about it?"

"What is there to do? He's leaving, or he's left by now, and that's it."

"But he is coming back?"

"He didn't say what he was doing for sure." Sarah's mind was still trying to understand what Kevan had said; why he left her like he had.

The food arrived and they took it outside to the picnic table. A soft breeze ruffled the napkins as they spread their food out on the picnic table between them.

Sarah looked at the food. "I don't think I can eat. My stomach's upset."

"Well, I'm starving." Cindy gave her a careful glance, her eyes narrowed in concern. "You don't look very good. Are you getting the flu or something?"

"I hope not. How am I going to tell my mom and dad? They are so excited that I am dating Kevan. Especially Mom."

"First, let's be sure he's left, that this isn't simply him doing a really awful job of dropping you."

"Kevan wouldn't do that. He wouldn't."

"How little you know of men, my innocent friend," Cindy said, delicately chewing a ketchup-covered French fry. "After a few more boyfriends you'll get the hang of it. Some are good, some not so good. And it looks like Kevan is about to be crowned prince of the not-so-good category."

"It's not like that, seriously," Sarah protested.

"Okay. If he was telling you the truth, when I call his house, he will not be there. Right?"

"How can you call the house when you don't know the number?"

"Have you forgotten that my dad is the head accountant at McElroy Manufacturing?"

"There's a pay phone right over there." Sarah pointed in the direction of the street corner. "Call away. I really don't care. If you're right and he just did a horrible job of dropping me, or if he's gone to Ireland as he said, I lose either way."

"We will get to the truth. You deserve that much." Cindy got up and went to the pay phone, pulling change from her evening bag as she opened the door to the booth.

Sarah could hear her speaking into the phone, her voice strong and determined. After a few minutes she glanced in Sarah's direction, her fingers tapping on the tiny counter in the booth. Sarah waited, wondering what was being said, but she was too worried to go over and listen in on the conversation.

In a few minutes Cindy returned, her gaze fixed on the picnic table. "I spoke to the housekeeper. She's a cousin of my mother's best friend, and you're right: Kevan is on his way to Boston to catch a flight to Ireland."

Sarah leaned across the table, nearly getting ketchup on her dress. "Did she say anything about how long he'd be away?"

Cindy shook her head. "She didn't seem to know anything else, and believe me I tried."

"Why did he leave me like this? He has to know how worried I'd be. What's going on?"

Cindy gave a sniff and straightened her shoulders. "His dad ordered him to leave. Tom McElroy is one mean man when he puts his mind to it. But you'll be okay, won't you? It's not like you're all alone, and after the way he left you I'd think twice about how this relationship is going. It was sexy and great in the beginning, but..." She shrugged.

Sarah fought to stem the flood of the tears, as waves of nausea overcame her. "I...I think I'm going to be—" She retched.

"Sarah! Let's get you into the car and home. Now!" Cindy grabbed her by the arm, and helped her to the car. She opened the door and pushed her into the seat. Sarah rolled down her window allowing the cool air to ease her stomach.

Cindy got into the driver's seat, her face wreathed with concern. "Sarah, I asked you one day about how far your relationship had gone with Kevan. You didn't answer. So I'm asking again now. Is there any chance you're pregnant?"

"What? No! I'm sick. That's all." In the midst of her emotional agony she remembered last night when Kevan had made love to her.

Cindy leaned across the bench seat of the car, looking like she had more to say.

"I must have the flu. I'll get you to drive me home and I'm going to bed."

"What will your mother think when she sees you home so soon? Are you ready to give her a long explanation about tonight?"

"I hadn't thought of that." She pushed her hair off her forehead. "I can't face my mother just yet."

"Why don't we sit in the car and talk a little bit? Maybe your mom will be asleep by the time I take you home."

Cindy rolled down her window and they sat in silence for a few minutes.

"Sarah, I have to say this because you are my best friend. I respect the fact that you may not want to tell me if you've had sex because you've never been good at talking about sex. But if there's any chance that you might be pregnant and with Kevan gone to Ireland, you need to think about what you'll do if you are pregnant. If you want, I'll go with you to get a pregnancy test kit. We could drive into Boston and get the kit so that no one will see us buy it. Your mom will never know."

"I'm not pregnant," Sarah said, stark fear starting to form a hard lump in her throat. "And even if I were, Kevan and I would love the baby, and make our life around him or her."

"Sarah, don't assume that Kevan would feel the way you do about a baby. He's got his whole life ahead of him. If his dad sent him to Ireland to work for the company, he may have other plans for his son. My dad says that Tom McElroy is very proud of Kevan, and plans for him to run the company one day. Did Kevan ever talk about what his father wanted him to do?"

"Not really."

"Then maybe you'd better focus on what you need, and not be so worried about him."

"Kevan left but he said he'd be in touch."

"Did he say when?" Cindy asked, her voice concerned.

"No. But I know he will."

"Sarah, I hate to be the one to say this, but there isn't a girl alive who hasn't, at one point or another, heard their boyfriend say something like that. Those are break-up words."

"No! Kevan did not break up with me!" Sarah said, close to tears as an image flashed in her mind of Kevan's face when he told her he was leaving.

"Sarah, get real. Kevan is the son of a man who will stop at nothing to get what he wants. You told me that his parents didn't know about you and Kevan. What if his father just found out in the last day or so, disapproved, and that's why Kevan has been sent to Ireland?"

Sarah balled her fists against the velvet folds of her dress. "That would be so cruel, so mean. But Kevan did say tonight that his father had found out…that he hadn't told them about us before."

Cindy nodded in sympathy. "If it were me, I would get a pregnancy test done. And if you are pregnant—"

"I'm not!"

"But if you are, you need to make plans about what you'll do. We're only a couple of months before our first term at Hastings. You're going to be a famous designer someday. And doing your degree, learning all you can, is the first step to making that dream come true. The last thing you need is an unwanted pregnancy."

"Stop talking that way! I don't know how you can talk about a baby like that. What's wrong with you?" she repeated, her voice rising.

Cindy tucked her hands in her lap. "Because I had an abortion last year."

Sarah gasped. "You *what*? When?"

"Remember I went away on spring break…?"

"You said you were going skiing in Colorado…"

"I went to a private clinic in California."

"Did your mom and dad know?"

"They paid for me to go." Cindy reached out and touched Sarah's hand where it rested on the seat. "We talked it over, and together we decided that I was too young to take on such responsibility."

"I can't believe this. You intentionally killed a baby? Just because you didn't want to look after a child? I would never do that. Never." She stared across the seat at the person she had felt closest to in the world. "You did that."

"I had no choice."

"Yes, you did." With that Sarah opened the car door. "You had a choice. If you didn't want a child, you could have put the baby up for adoption. How could you be my friend and do something like that? I'm going home."

"I'll drive you."

"No. You won't. I'll call my dad and he will pick me up."

CHAPTER FOUR

A few minutes later, Sarah saw her father's car edging along the street. She waved and the car pulled to the curb. Getting in, she was surprised to see her mom. "I thought Dad was going to pick me up," she said, leaning over to kiss her mother's cheek. The scent of her mother's face powder underscored the fact that Doris Maddison always put on makeup and dressed as if she were going out to lunch.

She patted Sarah's arm. "What are you doing out here on the street? Where is Kevan?" her mother asked.

Instinctively her fingers touched her throat where her locket had rested, causing her to shudder in dismay. She'd left the locket on the ground in the parking lot. Someone had probably driven over it and crushed it flat.

She felt sick all over again. "Can we talk about this later? I'm really tired."

"But this was your big night. You and Kevan going to your prom together." Her mother gave her a worried glance. "Everything's okay, isn't it?"

Not wanting to upset her mom, she searched for something to

say to distract her from asking questions that would only lead to more questions. "All those hours of decorating the gymnasium paid off. Everyone loved the tiny vases of lavender on the tables. And the sign I painted, especially the glitter paint, really looked great. And none of the balloons got loose and floated to the ceiling. Cindy and I..." She swallowed a sob.

"You and Cindy what?"

"We had a great time. But Doug came into the dance with her, and I think he'd been drinking."

Her mother drove carefully along the winding street leading to their house. "I'm so glad you don't drink," her mother said. "So many teenagers do these days. Your father and I were remarking over dinner this evening how proud we are of you, how you've never given us a moment of worry. I hear so many of my friends talk about their daughters being sassy, going out and staying out past their curfew. I know it's the seventies, and everyone is having free everything, and girls go out dressed like harlots but still..."

Her mother sighed. "And just the other day Pamela Denning was telling me that her niece has been skipping school the last two months, and playing pool of all things. I don't know what is going on with teenagers today. I'm just so glad that you're a good girl, a good daughter. No one could accuse you of sleeping around or drinking. I don't understand these young women."

Sarah's cheeks felt hot, her throat dry as sawdust. What should she do? She'd have to tell her mom sooner or later what happened earlier in the evening, and why Kevan hadn't driven her home.

They drove for a few more minutes, and still her mother said nothing about why Sarah had been waiting at the burger place. It wasn't a pool hall but it was hardly a place for her to be hanging out in the most expensive dress she'd ever owned.

Knowing her words would upset her mother, she decided to tell her before they got home. "Mom, Kevan has gone to Ireland."

"He's what?" Her mother swerved to the curb, the wash of the headlights illuminating a billboard showing a handsome rancher smoking a Camel cigarette.

Her mother pushed the gearshift on the steering column into park, and turned to Sarah. "I knew something was up. You waiting at a burger place on prom night. Tell me what's going on."

She explained what had happened, her voice failing her at the memory of those last moments she'd shared with Kevan. She glanced over at her mother.

"Kevan didn't say when he's coming home again. Did Dad hear anyone say anything at the plant?" she asked, hoping that one of the men on the production line might have said something. Kevan had been working after school at the plant to learn the business.

"I can't believe that Tom McElroy's son would do such a thing. Imagine leaving you to face your classmates and to have to explain why you and he weren't together at the prom."

She waited for her mother to say something more, something encouraging about how she could spend her free time while she waited for Kevan to come home. She was so thankful that she hadn't had a drink of liquor from the brown paper bags that some of her classmates had offered. If she'd gotten into the car smelling of alcohol her mother would have been even more upset.

"I'm sorry this had to happen. I can see why you and Cindy wanted to get away from there. The two of you didn't have a very nice prom night, and I'm truly sorry." Her mother glanced over at her and Sarah saw the genuine concern on her face. "That young man needs to be told to behave like a man, that it's not okay to do something like this to you. He knows better than to behave like that."

Sarah let out the breath she'd been holding. She wanted to cry with relief but knew that her mother would simply give her a gentle scolding about how tears wouldn't do any good.

"Thanks Mom. I'm sure Kevan will call me tomorrow from

Ireland. He didn't know how long he'd be away, but he'll be back as soon as he can, I'm sure."

She'd never been less sure of anything in her life.

CHAPTER FIVE

The next morning and for days after Sarah didn't talk to Cindy. She pretended to have the flu so her mother wouldn't ask any more questions, and she stayed home from school so she wouldn't see Cindy. She knew she would have to face her friend, and try to understand why she'd had an abortion, but for now, she needed time away from her.

When she'd told her mother she was ill, her mother got her a doctor's appointment. She'd go if she had to, but in the meantime, her thoughts were on Kevan. She wanted to be near the phone, should he call; another reason for pretending to be ill. Her cat, Patches, a black and white tabby, offered her the only comfort she had as she waited to hear from him, the hours and days dragging on and on.

She stared up at the ceiling and wondered where Kevan was right now. It was at least five hours later in Ireland, wasn't it? That would mean he would be having lunch, or maybe enjoying a sunny day in the city, or maybe he had convinced his dad to let him come back.

Her mother arrived home from her clerical job at McElroy

Manufacturing in the afternoon. Placing her purse and scarf on the hall rack with her coat, she came into the living room where Sarah sat watching All My Children. "It seems that Tom has sent Kevan to work in the European office where he is to be part of an acquisition team to buy up companies in Ireland and Europe as part of their expansion plans. No one seems to think that Kevan is coming back any time soon."

"But he hasn't graduated high school yet," Sarah protested. "What would he have to offer? He told me he doesn't know anything about the business side of the company, and that's why his dad had him working his summer vacations for the past three years. But those jobs were on the production floor." A feeling of loss, fear and loneliness swept through Sarah. "Mom, what am I going to do? I love him."

"Now, dear, you don't have any control over what is going on in Kevan's life. You will simply have to wait and see. In the meantime, you have to look after your own life. You've got a great future waiting for you at Hastings. Your dad and I couldn't be prouder."

"But I want Kevin here with me. How will I survive the summer without him?"

"You just have to be patient. Things will work out for the best."

At the thought of being alone all summer, Sarah began to cry.

Her mother settled next to her on the sofa. "Now. Now. Try not to think about it."

"I can't help myself," Sarah sobbed.

Her mother held her close, smoothing Sarah's hair away from her face. "Sarah, try to understand that Kevan may not be back anytime soon."

"You don't know that!"

"No. I don't. But I do know he has to do what his father tells him to do."

"But, what about me? How could he leave me like this? We had so many plans."

"We don't always get what we want my darling. If we did you would be one of four children."

She stared into her mother's eyes and saw the truth of her words. "You couldn't have more children? I'm so sorry, Mom. I thought that you'd decided not to have more children after me."

Her mother shook her head slowly. "Your father and I had actually picked out the names of three girls and three boys just in case we were lucky enough to have more babies."

Sarah hugged her mother close. "Oh, Mom, I love you so much."

CHAPTER SIX

Two months later

After Kevan had left, Sarah felt as if time stood still. She didn't feel the same about anything anymore. She'd gone into Harrison's Drugstore to pick up her last pay check and was on her way back home when she heard Cindy call out: "Sarah, wait up," Cindy raced down the steps of Harrison's Drugstore. "Where are you going in such a hurry?"

Cindy's blue shorts fit her slim body perfectly, though Sarah thought her matching blue top showed too much cleavage. But Sarah recognized that these thoughts were jealous thoughts. Her own days of prancing around in short shorts wouldn't be happening any day soon.

Cindy's carefree attitude, once so appealing, now grated on Sarah's nerves. Sarah hadn't known a carefree moment since Kevan had left for Ireland. She felt terrible about the argument she'd had with Cindy all those long weeks ago, but there was no way to take the words back now.

She had managed to get through her graduation ceremony

without Kevan, and without breaking down and crying in front of her entire class. She'd gone home afterward with her parents and had been home pretty well ever since her doctor's appointment when she learned that she was expecting a baby.

With Kevan gone she felt totally alone. Instead of making plans for Hastings, she'd spent every waking hour trying to figure out what had driven Kevan away, and why he hadn't been in touch with her. She had tried to get in touch with him, but the housekeeper refused to take a message.

"Cindy, I can't talk right now. I have to get home."

She couldn't ask for Cindy's help without telling her the truth about her situation. And she couldn't do that, not only because of the fight they'd had, but because they would be going their separate ways this fall. Looking at her friend, Sarah wished with all her heart that life had not turned out the way it did.

"Please wait. I need to talk to you. I'm sorry about the fight we had. I should have told you about...California. I have Dad's car, Sarah. Let me drive you home."

Sarah saw the worry in Cindy's eyes, and nearly relented. "I have to get home."

"Why won't you talk to me?"

"I'm really busy right now." The excuse slipped out so easily.

Cindy grabbed her arm. "What's wrong with you?" she demanded. "You haven't returned any of my calls. I went by the other night, and your mother said you weren't feeling well. What's the matter," Cindy insisted, concern showing in her eyes.

Sarah wanted to wrap her arms around her friend and sob out her story, to have Cindy offer sympathy and understanding when she confided how her life had changed forever. Of all the people in her life, Cindy would be the one person who might understand what she was going through. But shame held her back. "Nothing's wrong. I'm fine."

"I thought you trusted me."

"I do. But I have to get home."

"So when can we talk?"

Sarah met Cindy's anxious gaze, aware that in a few days she would be leaving and probably wouldn't see Cindy again for a very long time. "I don't know," she said. She had promised her parents that she would keep quiet about what was going on in her life, about expecting a baby, and that Kevan had not been in touch to take responsibility.

She would never forget the look of shock and grief in her parents' eyes when she told them about the results of her pregnancy test. Determined to save face, her parents had spent hours searching for a place she could live while she waited to have her baby, somewhere out of town, away from her friends and the curious concerned looks of their neighbors.

"I'm leaving tomorrow," she said, shocked at the fear that ambushed her as she said the words out loud.

"You're going to Hastings early?" Cindy eyes widened in question.

Sarah had had to notify the university that she wouldn't be attending this fall, and it had been the hardest call she'd ever made. "No, I'm going into nurse's training in Bangor."

"Seriously? When did you decide to do that?"

It was the lie she'd agreed to tell when people asked. Bangor was far enough away that people would probably not check up on her, and by the time they did, she'd actually be living in Bar Harbor with her aunt and uncle.

"Why would you give up your dream of being a designer?"

The genuine concern in Cindy's eyes made Sarah feel so lonely. How she wished for those carefree days when she and her friend spent hours talking about clothes and boys. "It's what I want."

"I don't believe you, Sarah Maddison. I know how much you wanted to go to Hastings."

Sarah's eyes stung with unshed tears. "Things change."

As they stood facing each other, tears trickled down Cindy's cheeks. The look on her face was so sad, so filled with longing that Sarah started to cry too.

"Why are you doing this, Sarah?" Cindy asked. "Is it because of the argument we had?"

Afraid that her friend might put her arms around her, she stepped back a little. Shaking her head, she swallowed to fight off the agony filling her heart. "I...I've changed my plans, that's all."

Cindy slipped one hand into the pocket of her shorts. "Dad told me that Kevan is in Ireland and isn't coming back for a while. Knowing how bad you must be feeling I wanted to help you, but if this is how it's going to be between us..." She gave a hopeless shrug. "I brought you something." She held out her hand. The locket Kevan had given Sarah glistened in the sunlight. "Someone found this in the school parking lot, and turned into the lost and found. I was at the school with my brother the other day, and they were cleaning the box out when I spotted it. It's yours, isn't it?"

Numb with relief, Sarah nodded. She turned it over in her hand, her heart thundering loud in her chest. Struggling to control her despair, Sarah wrapped her arms around her friend. "Thank you so much. You have no idea what this means to me. I'll never forget you."

Cindy hugged her back. "You'd better not," she said.

"And I'm sorry I can't talk to you. I want us to be friends again, but I...I'll call you as soon as I can."

"Double promise?" Cindy's smile trembled.

"Double promise." Clutching the locket to her heart Sarah turned and walked away, not trusting herself to look back at her childhood friend. A heaviness engulfed her as she started the long walk back to her house. She would never understand how Kevan could abandon her to a life in Bar Harbor without him.

CHAPTER SEVEN

*H*alf an hour later, Sarah reached the safety of her back door.

"Is that you, honey?" her mother asked, holding the phone out to Sarah as she entered the narrow hall from the kitchen. "It's for you," she said.

"Who is it?"

Placing her hand over the receiver, her mother whispered, "I don't recognize the voice, but she sounds anxious." She gave Sarah the faintest of smiles. "I'll be in the kitchen when you're done."

Sarah slid onto the tiny needlepoint-covered chair beside the hall table. "Hello."

"Hi, Sarah. This is Julia, Kevan's sister."

Sarah gasped. "Is Kevan back home? Is he okay? Can I speak with him?" she asked, hope charging through her.

"No, he's still in Ireland. He called here last night, and I took the call. My parents were out. He told me he was really sorry for how he left you."

"What else did he say? Is he going to call me? I need to speak with him."

"He's hoping to be back home soon, and he wanted me to tell you to wait for him, that this will all get sorted out when he gets back."

Sarah closed her eyes, remembering those last hours before he left. "Do you know when he'll be home?"

"No. He didn't say. I don't think he knows for sure."

"Do you have a phone number for him?"

"Sarah, I can't do that."

"Why not? I really need to talk to him."

"If Dad finds out I talked to Kevan, there'll be trouble."

Sarah wanted to be sympathetic to Julia, but right now she needed Kevan. "Julia, please give me his number. Please."

"Sarah, I have to go. If my father finds out I've been talking to you about Kevan he will be furious."

"I don't get it. Why is your father so upset?"

"Because I helped Kevan keep his relationship with you a secret."

She waited anxious to know about Kevan, anything about him that would tell her he loved her. "What did he say about me?"

"Kevan wanted to warn you not to let your parents talk to Dad about you and him. If they do, my father will call in the loan the company holds on your house, and your parents' jobs could be... they could be fired. Your parents would lose their house."

Sarah cried out in disbelief. "Your father wouldn't do that! Why would he want to hurt my dad that way? He's always been a good worker for the company. My mom really wants to keep her job. How could he be like that?"

"I was listening at the door when I heard him yelling at Kevan about you. Sarah, I can't talk any longer. I have to go before the housekeeper finds me on the phone. If anyone tells my father I talked to you—"

A thought slid through her mind. "Did Kevan fall?"

"Fall?" Julia sniffled. "Why would you ask?"

"The night he left Kevan said he'd fallen and hurt his ribs."

"I don't think so… I'm sure he would have told me if he had."

Then had Kevan's father hit him during an argument? If his dad did strike Kevan, she could only imagine how frightened he must have been. How she wished she could talk with him.

Sarah heard someone's strident voice in the background. "I have to go, but don't forget what I said," Julia whispered.

"I won't." Sarah hung up the phone her mind a jumbled mess of thoughts, mingled with a yearning for Kevan that forced tears to her eyes. All of it made her feel ill. She clutched her tummy, willing herself to concentrate on what to do next.

For now, she would focus on getting her packing finished and moving to her aunt and uncle's in Bar Harbor, until all of this got straightened out. She and Kevan were going to be parents. It wasn't how she had imagined the arrival of their first baby. But once she and Kevan were able to make plans for the future, it would all work out.

With hope easing her worried thoughts, Sarah went to the kitchen. "Can I help with supper, Mom?"

"Who was that on the phone?" Her mother's expression was one Sarah had come to recognize – that of concern mixed with anxiety.

"Just a friend." She wouldn't tell her what Julia has said, not unless she had to. Knowing that the man her father had worked for all his life could be so cruel, so vindictive, would only add to her parents' anxiety.

When her parents had first learned that she was dating Kevan they were thrilled, excited over the possibility that their daughter would marry someone as socially prominent as Kevan McElroy, son of Tom McElroy and heir to McElroy Manufacturing. Her mother had talked of nothing else in the weeks leading up to the prom. Excited talk about how they'd be making wedding plans someday.

Despite their disappointment in the past weeks, her parents had pitched in and arranged for her to go and live in Bar Harbor with her dad's sister. Tomorrow she was leaving town, getting away from all the trouble she'd caused.

"Come with me," her mother said. Her lips were pursed, her shoulders stiff and straight. "There is something that needs to be taken care of before you go tomorrow."

Sarah followed her mother to the den, an austere room with narrow windows, framed by heavy beige drapes against a backdrop of pearl-grey walls. She hoped that whatever her mother had to say wouldn't take long as she had a lot of packing to do before she left tomorrow. Her thoughts went to her conversation with Cindy and how she hoped to be able to talk to her friend someday soon. When this was all over, and she and Kevan were settled, Cindy would be the first person invited to their tiny apartment. If they had a girl she intended to call her Cindy.

"Sit down." Her mother nodded to a chair by the window that looked out onto the vegetable garden so carefully tended by her father.

"What is it, Mom?"

"Your father and I have talked it over. We feel you should give your baby up for adoption so that you can continue your career. Perhaps they'll agree to extend the offer of a scholarship if it's only a year..."

"What!" Shock slammed into Sarah's heart. "Give up my baby? I can't give my baby away to strangers. I can't—"

"Sarah, I realize that right now this is all so new for you, that you probably believe that Kevan will come back into your life, and the two of you will marry and raise your child together."

"Sure I do. Kevan had to leave but he'll be back," she said with a lot more certainty than she felt.

"But what if he doesn't? What if he denies that this baby is his? He wouldn't be the first man to deny responsibility for a child. And if he does, how will you support yourself and your baby? "

Sarah stared at her mother, her mind struggling to understand what her mother was telling her. Did her mother really believe that Kevan would turn his back on his child?

"Sarah, you have to face facts. You cannot support a child on your own."

"I'll get a job. I'll save money. Mom, I can't give up my baby."

"Sarah, without any money from the father of your child, how do you expect to raise your baby? We'll help you where we can, but you'll need a lot of support and raising a child on your own will be expensive. I wish things were different. I wish Kevan was man enough to look after you and your unborn child."

"Mom, you told me you always wanted to have more children. You must be able to understand how it feels to have the chance for a child. I have this chance. The circumstances aren't the best, but Kevan and I will find a way. Mom, you can't mean what you just said. And I don't believe Dad agreed to this."

"He did. It's all we've talked about for the past few days. You have to wake up and see what has happened to you. You're expecting a baby with no husband to support you."

She swallowed hard against the wave of panic coursing through her. What *would* she do if Kevan didn't come back?

"Mom, Kevan had to go to Ireland because his father needed him to be there. He won't be gone long. When he gets back we will make our plans to care for our baby. Things will work out. You'll see. I realize that having me here under the circumstances is difficult for you, and I'm happy to go to my aunt and uncle's house until Kevan returns."

"Sarah, it's time you faced reality," her mother said, pacing the floor. "Things are not going to work out, or that poor excuse of a man would be here with you, or have called to say when he's coming back. If Kevan doesn't marry you, and if you won't agree to put the baby up for adoption, your father and I will contact Tom McElroy. He can well afford to help out here."

"No. Oh, no, please don't do that."

"I went back to work so that you could have a university education, make a life for yourself, be the first person in my family to get an education. I did it so that you would have a better life than your father and I had. If you keep your baby without Kevan's support, you will live to regret it. You will struggle to raise your child; it will put an end to your career plans, and you'll end up marrying someone just to make ends meet. That's not what we worked so hard for."

For the first time since she'd learned she was pregnant, Sarah was truly scared. What if she did have to struggle for years to care for her child? Would she be able to do it?

"Please, Mom, I just need a chance to sort everything out. I can't decide about adoption right this minute, especially without hearing from Kevan. It wouldn't be fair to my baby or to me. I need more time."

"Time? You don't have time. You have to get to Bar Harbor and find a job for a few months. You have to do your part to help us out. Your father and I will talk it over with your aunt and uncle, and figure out the best way to find a family for your child."

"You don't really mean that. Mom, please don't do this."

"Sarah, we will help you as much as we can, but you have to smarten up where Kevan is concerned. If you don't, all your plans for your future will be over. No college. No career. Nothing. Just caring for a child alone while you try to find a job to pay for babysitting and putting food on the table. Meanwhile the man who got you into this mess goes his merry way, enjoying a carefree life of fun and privilege."

"Mom, Kevan isn't like that. Besides, it's the seventies. Women have babies and a career," Sarah protested, but even to her ears it sounded hollow. How would she manage without Kevan's support?

"Well, Kevan's father can help out with the bills. That's all I'm saying."

Sarah couldn't listen any longer. Somehow, she had to stop her mother from rushing over to the McElroy mansion and confronting Tom McElroy about his son. She knew her mother would demand that he be brought back from Ireland, something that would only happen when Kevan's father agreed to do it.

All her mother would accomplish would be to guarantee that they'd lose their home. "Mom, that was Julia, Kevan's sister, on the phone."

Her mother's expression lightened. "Why didn't you tell me this before? What did she say? Did you get an address or phone number for Kevan?"

"No. I didn't. Julia told me that she overheard her dad saying that if you or Dad tried to interfere in his family's issues, he will call the loan on this house."

The air hissed through her mother's lips. "Sarah, Tom McElroy wouldn't do any such thing. Your father's a good worker, has been with the company for nearly twenty years."

"It's not about Dad, or the fact that he's a good employee. It's about you and Dad staying out of Kevan's life."

"If Tom McElroy is willing to call our loan, he'd be willing to keep Kevan in Ireland. It tells me that his son had no intention of ever coming back to you or your baby," her mother said, her eyes dark, her face pale.

Fear wrapped its tentacles around Sarah's heart, slowing her breath. "I'll wait to hear from Kevan. I'll get a job, and I will make a life for the two of us until he returns."

Her mother sighed, her arms going around Sarah's shoulders. "Listen to me. You can't come back from Bar Harbor without a father for your child. I know what I'm talking about. If your father hadn't agreed to marry me when I found out I was expecting, you wouldn't have had the life you have now."

"You were pregnant with me before you were married?" Sarah asked.

"I was. But it was different for me. Your dad didn't run off and leave me. We got married and no one knew. When you were born I told everyone that you were a few weeks early. No one said anything. It was how things were done. We may be living in the seventies, but nothing has changed when it comes to the realities of having a child. I don't want you to face what I might have faced if your father hadn't done the right thing."

CHAPTER EIGHT

*H*olding the cat carrier with a squirming Patches inside, Sarah fought back tears as she stood looking at the only home she'd ever known. The maple tree where her father helped her carve her initials when she was six, the delphiniums waving their flowering heads, the carefully mown front law with its winding foot path leading to the front porch where large pots of red geraniums framed the door. "Mom, I hope Aunt Elsie and Uncle Fred don't mind me bringing Patches."

"They don't mind. I talked to them, and they are excited to have you stay with them. They've actually talked to a local restaurant owner, a client of your uncle's accounting business, and he is willing to hire you right away."

"But I have no restaurant experience," Sarah said, dreading the thought that she wouldn't be coming back here for months. She'd never been away from home like this.

"You don't have to worry. Your uncle has looked after everything for you. They want you to be as happy as possible while you're living with them."

Her mother hugged her. "And if I hear anything at all about Kevan I'll let you know. He may come through yet, and do the right thing," her mother said consolingly.

"He will. You'll see," Sarah said, trying to sound upbeat.

Her father finished putting her suitcases and a couple of boxes of design books in the trunk. "We'd better get on the road," he said, coming around the car and taking Sarah's hand. "This will all work out for you, I promise."

"Dad, I don't want to go. I can't do this alone, without someone," she pleaded.

Her father pulled her into his arms. "We're here if you need us. We'll come to visit you as often as we can. Mom will bring some of her molasses cookies." He pulled back and took her shoulders in his powerful hands. "It's the best we can do for now," he said, choking on the words. "Let's get going."

The three of them got into the car. Sarah put the cat carrier on her lap and tried to calm Patches. The cat kept putting its paws through the open spaces in the crate, mewling in misery. Crying silently, Sarah watched all the familiar places move past the car window: the Episcopalian church where she'd gone every Sunday for as long as she could remember, the park where she'd spent hours reading during the summer, Harrison's Drugstore, the last place she'd seen Cindy.

Hours later, when they pulled into the driveway in Bar Harbor, they immediately spotted her aunt and uncle sitting on the verandah of the colonial-style house. "I'll get your suitcases. You go see Fred and Elsie," her father said.

Her aunt and uncle came down the driveway toward her. Aunt Elsie, a tall woman with gray hair that flowed around her shoulders, held out her arms. "It's been a long time since you've visited with us, dear. And we're so glad you're going to live here for a little while."

"I'm glad to be here, Aunt Elsie," Sarah said, as her aunt

embraced her. The scent of lavender wafted around her. She said the words to please her aunt and her parents, but she didn't mean any of them. She wanted to go home.

"Come on into the house while I get lunch on the table." Elsie glanced around. "Where's Patches? That's your cat's name, right?"

"Still in the car. I'll get him," Sarah said, thankful to have something to focus on other than the storm of emotions charging through her. *What if she was too homesick to stay there? What would happen then?* Reaching into the car for Patches made her realize how bloated she was feeling…

Carrying the carrier to the front door was awkward, made worse by the loud howls coming from the crate. "I think he may need his litter box," she said, apologizing for her cat.

"We've already got one set up in the laundry room." Her aunt led her into the back of the house. "There. Will that work?" She pointed to the square plastic box filled with litter.

"It's perfect. Thank you for doing this," Sarah said, feeling tears pressing against her eyelids as she placed the carrier on the floor and opened the door for Patches.

"I understand how you must be feeling right now," her aunt said, taking her hands. "But it's going to get better, I promise. Fred and I never had children and we are really looking forward to having you with us. And we are so pleased that you brought Patches with you. I had a cat once, a huge tabby with big ears. I loved that cat so much. Trust me. I know why you had to bring him along."

Sarah put her arms around her aunt and sobbed into her neck, her body shaking. "I…I don't know if I can do this."

"You must, my darling. Your parents are counting on it. They want you to be happy, that's all. Have you heard from this Kevan person?" her aunt asked.

"Not yet." Sarah sniffed and searched the room for her cat. Patches was squatting in the litter box, and seeing him doing something so ordinary and natural made her smile for the first time since she she'd woken up that morning.

A few minutes later, Sarah sat eating and listening to her parents and her aunt and uncle talking about things that didn't matter to her, her thoughts on how she would survive living there alone. As she looked at her parents, the anxiety on their faces faintly disguised by the forced smiles and over-loud talk made her wish that she could have saved them from all this emotional pain.

When her father got up, he turned to her. "We have to get back," he said, his voice thick. "Your mother and I will miss you."

Sarah stood up and hugged her dad so tight the buttons on his jacket hurt as they pressed into her. "I'll be all right. I will," she said, forcing her voice to remain upbeat.

She walked to the car with them, each step a kind of torture. Her desperate need for them became a looming fear that once they were gone, she would not see them for weeks. They hugged her tight between them. "When this is all over, we'll have a family vacation," her mother said.

Sarah couldn't say that any vacation from there on would include her child. She couldn't say that her only reason for being here was to have her baby, and find a life that would allow her to raise her child. She couldn't say any of it because she'd said it all before and no one listened.

She watched them leave, her heart heavy, her body aching from the long drive, and now filled with fear that she would not sleep tonight because of her loneliness. She went back into the house; to the too-bright smiles of her new family. To a life she never wanted, but was forced to accept.

Yet, as they smiled at her, she realized that free of her parents' constant concern for her she would be able to come up with a plan for her and her baby's future – a future she prayed with all her heart – that would include Kevan.

Patches mewed as he stretched and blinked his eyes in sleepiness. At least she had her cat, and in a few weeks Kevan would be with her, and they would work out their problems together.

She picked Patches up and held him close, his soft purrs so reassuring.

"Mom says you know of a restaurant where I might be able to get a job," she said, with all the courage she could muster.

CHAPTER NINE

*T*wo days later, Sarah walked along the tourist-clogged streets looking for Patterson's Steak and Seafood Restaurant. Elsie had offered to drive her, but she wanted to do this on her own. If this was to be her life she would have to learn to fend for herself. She'd been told by her aunt and uncle that Benjamin Patterson was a very caring man, that she could rely on him to treat her with respect.

Whether or not he was caring didn't really matter as long as he was willing to employ her as a waitress. She spotted the front of the restaurant and the sandwich board outside displaying the specials of the day. She was about to open the door when four couples streamed out, laughing and talking amongst themselves.

Inside, Sarah found herself facing a lineup in front of a sign encouraging people to wait to be seated. Glancing around the milling crowd she wondered if any of the men she could see behind the bar might be her potential new boss.

Finally, it was her turn.

"I'm Sarah Maddison. I'm here to see Mr. Patterson about a job," she said, anxious to appear professional.

The girl stopped and looked her over, before picking up the phone. "Tell Benjamin the new hire is here. Sarah Maddison," she said, before hanging up and offering Sarah a distracted smile. "I'm sure he'll be right along," she said, looking behind Sarah at the next party waiting for a table.

Sarah moved to the side, taking in the dark wood, the low light levels and the haphazard arrangement of paintings done by local artists. There was so much she could do with this restaurant. Arranging the paintings would add a different feel – more color would be good too.

She was still looking at the restaurant space when a man walked toward her. He had a lovely smile, and although he was dressed casually, his clothes fit him well. He was what Cindy would have called a hunk, but she shouldn't think of her potential new boss that way.

Was this Benjamin Patterson?

She waited as his gaze swept over her. She caught herself hoping he was.

BENJAMIN'S DAY had started at four am with a call from his security company saying that an alarm had gone off inside the restaurant. By the time they called back to say there was nothing to worry about, he'd already showered and dressed for the busy day that lay ahead.

Last evening he'd talked to his sister, Lilly, who fretted out loud that he wasn't getting any younger, that he'd had lots of girlfriends, but never had come close to a permanent relationship. Lilly was very clear in what she thought his problem was: He couldn't open up and share his feelings.

He would have ignored his sister, except for the fact that the last woman he'd dated had said the same thing. Yet, he argued with his sister that she was wrong, even though a part of what she said could be true. *But, what did women expect from a busy man like him? And if they were so concerned about how he felt why did they insist upon talking about themselves all the time?*

Distractedly he glanced at the young woman waiting for him near the door.

She was a knockout with her sun-streaked hair and beautiful sea-green eyes that seemed to look straight through him. He guessed her to be about eighteen. He'd agreed to consider her as a member of the wait staff at his accountant's request, but just looking at her, the uncertain way she toyed with the strap on her purse, made him wonder if he was doing the right thing. She didn't seem to have much in the way of work experience, and if he spent the money to train her, and she decided she didn't like it there...

"Miss Maddison, I'm Benjamin Patterson, owner of Patterson's Steak and Seafood Restaurant." He held out his hand, directing her to walk with him among the tables over to the stairs leading to his office. "We can talk up here, if that's okay with you." Without waiting for her to answer he opened his office door and beckoned her to enter.

Once behind his desk, he searched for the scrap of paper where he'd written down the information on this young woman... Giving up the search, he covered his discomfort with a smile and said, "Why don't you tell me about yourself, your work experience and why you want to work at my restaurant?"

She crossed one leg over the other, her narrow skirt sliding up her thigh. Placing her hands firmly in her lap, she said, "I am living with my aunt and uncle while I find a job here in Bar Harbor."

"Why did you move here? And where are you from?" he asked.

"I'm from Waltham, near Boston. I moved here to—" She coughed and pulled the edges of her skirt down. "I worked during school at the local pharmacy in my neighborhood. I stocked shelves and worked at the counter. I had a full scholarship to Hastings to study design." She glanced at the ceiling, her eyes shimmering, words failing her.

He sighed inwardly. The last thing he needed was a troubled young woman who regretted her move there. "Miss Maddison, I didn't mean to upset you. Please." He handed her a box of tissue from his desk drawer.

"I'm really sorry for this." She wiped her eyes, and scrunched the tissue in her hand. "I want you to know that I really want this job. If I get it I won't let you or my uncle down. I promise."

He saw the anxiety in her eyes, and decided not to push her further. He'd agreed to offer her a job, but she probably wouldn't stay long once she realized how hard waitress work was.

"Okay. You can start tomorrow. Today I need you to go to the payroll clerk in the office next door and do the paperwork necessary for employment here, then down to the staff room to find a uniform. I'll expect you here tomorrow morning at 7:00. You'll be assigned to a waitress who will train you."

She clapped her hands together, her smile wide, her eyes gleaming as her hair framed her face in a way that made her look sexy and at the same time vulnerable. "Thank you so much," she said.

As their eyes met he felt something shift in his chest. He held her gaze while his heart pounded, his mouth went dry and he couldn't think of one sane thing to say to her. He settled for, "That's it, then. See you tomorrow."

He watched her walk away from him toward the door, the easy movement of her body, the way she'd glanced back at him with that look of appreciation in her eyes, made him thankful she was out of his line of vision.

He tapped his pen on the desk, waiting for his pulse to settle back, waiting for the rush of attraction to ease. How could it be that of all the women he'd dated, he had this sense of connection with this woman he didn't know, had never met before? Yet this bond felt real, as if it had been there for a very long time.

"Give your head a shake, Patterson," he said to the empty room. "You're at least ten years older than her, and hopefully wiser."

CHAPTER TEN

On the walk home Sarah wanted to skip along the sidewalk. She was the happiest she'd been since Kevan left for Ireland. She had her uniform tucked in a paper bag, and she would wash and iron it when she got back to the house. She was going to be a full-time employee of Patterson's Steak and Seafood Restaurant, the words emblazoned on her uniform, and she was certain she could learn to do the job and do it well.

When she went in the back door her aunt and uncle were waiting for her.

"How did it go?" her Uncle Fred asked, taking the bag from her.

"What's this?" Elsie asked.

"It's my uniform. I start tomorrow morning at 7:00."

"That's great news!" With a hoot of laughter Fred danced her around the kitchen, in an exaggerated waltz step, coming to stop in front of the table. "We are going to celebrate tonight. Elsie sent me down to the butcher's shop for a top sirloin. I got a few new potatoes and carrots, and ice cream for dessert. Does Patches like ice cream?"

"Fred," Elsie said in mock disgust. "Cats don't ice cream."

"They eat cream, don't they?" He winked at Sarah. "Okay. So, the next order of business is that I fire up the charcoal and we get this party underway."

An hour later Fred was outside barbequing the steak while Sarah helped Elsie cut up vegetables and set the table. "This job means so much to me, Aunt Elsie. I'll be able to pay rent to you."

Elsie turned to her. "You do not pay rent in this house. I want you to save your money so you can do the things you'll need to do once this is over."

Did this mean her aunt might not agree with her mother? *Dare she hope it might be possible?* She went about setting the table with renewed vigor, going through the sideboard drawers looking for just the right placemats. She found a set with beautiful gold and green flowers on a cream background. She held them up. "Can I use these?"

"You certainly can," Elsie said, chopping the vegetables for coleslaw.

"Aunt Elsie, do you have candles I could put on the table?"

Elsie glanced over, a huge smile on her face. "Do you remember the time you came here to visit, and you asked me the same thing. You said you wanted to make things pretty. I remember that visit so well. You were supposed to stay overnight with us, you and your family. Then your dad got a call about something going on at work, and he had to go back. Fred and I were going to keep you overnight and drive you back home the next day. When it came time for your parents to leave, you acted all brave, but before they pulled out of the yard you pleaded to go with them. Do you remember that?"

Her thoughts swerved to her parents, to her home and all that she missed. She couldn't let herself think about any of that. "I do. I was twelve, wasn't I?"

"Yeah, all grown up you said, when Fred teased you." Elsie came to stand next to her. "We've always loved you. If we'd been able to have a daughter we would have wanted her to be just like you. As for what is going on in your life right now, honey, it will all work out. You'll see. You just need to have faith that we will find a good home for your baby."

If only Kevan were with her...

"You are giving up your baby, aren't you?" Elsie asked, a small frown forming between her eyes. "Your mother said you were..."

Why would her mother say that after the argument they'd had? Yet, looking at her aunt and her open warmth, she realized that she couldn't talk about her baby for now. Tomorrow, she would use the pay phone outside the restaurant, call Kevan's house and get a phone number she could call. She had to believe that Kevan would want to know he was going to be a father.

THE MORNING SKY was a splash of bright blue fringed with puffs of white cloud. Sarah had barely slept once she'd made up her mind to call Kevan's house. But she had a lot to do before she could make a call to anyone. Threading her way between the early morning tourists out enjoying the salt air, she arrived at the staff entrance of Patterson's Steak and Seafood Restaurant. As she reached for the door one of the women she'd met yesterday was holding it open.

"Wow! That uniform looks great on you. The aquamarine color is perfect with your hair." She followed Sarah inside. "So, it's your first day at work. Are you excited?"

"I am."

"And you've been assigned to Leslie Anne Taylor. She's great. Everyone here is great to work with. I've worked in a lot of restaurants along the east coast and this one is really nice." She leaned close in a conspiratorial way. "If Benjamin Patterson ever looked my way, you know the way I'm talking about, I would literally fall into his arms. Isn't he gorgeous? And he isn't married. Never has been. The scuttlebutt is that he is really kind and generous with the women in his life. He dotes on his mother. He has a sister, Lilly, who is a nurse and works in New York."

"He sounds perfect," she said.

Leslie Anne came up to her. "It's great to meet you, Sarah. We have a lot to do this morning before the place fills for breakfast." She moved ahead of her into the main restaurant area. "Let's get started. I have my usual assignment of tables, and you will work with me. Have you had any experience waiting tables?"

"No. Unless you count serving people at the strawberry festival at my church each year."

Leslie Anne's eyes lit up, as a smile spread across her face. "Not quite the same...but it will help. Come with me and let's get started."

SARAH WORKED HARD, trying to take in everything she needed to know about waiting on tables. By four o'clock her feet were so sore she could hardly stand, and her back ached. Several staff members arrived to start the evening shift while Sarah continued to follow Leslie Anne's lead on folding napkins at a table near the back.

"The evenings are always busy. Some of us will work until 6:00 to help cover the dinner crowd. One of the waiters always brings the sandwich board in from outside once lunch is over, and if we get a free minute we put the specials on it. None of us has much skill in making it look interesting or inviting but we do the best we can." Leslie Anne shifted her weight from one foot to the other. "It's my turn to do it tonight before I leave."

Sarah looked at the board, with its chalkboard surface and scrawled writing. "I could do that, if you'd like. All I need are some pieces of different colored chalk and the list of the specials."

Leslie Anne looked at her with interest. "That would be nice. Have you done this before?"

"No. But I took art lessons, and I love to design things. If it's okay with you, I'll finish the napkins, then do the board before I leave. You'll tell me what you think, if I need to make any changes. How's that?"

"Works for me." Leslie Anne got up, stretched her back and went to the cook for the specials. Returning, she passed the colored chalk and specials list to Sarah. "Can't wait to see what you do with this. Maybe we have an artist amongst us."

Sarah settled in and went to work. She loved sketching, working the words into the spaces, highlighting some of them, making everything readable. She was just finishing up when she spotted Benjamin talking earnestly to Leslie Anne.

A little anxious she watched him make his way around tables and behind booths to where she was sitting with the sandwich board.

"Let me see what you've done," he said, his voice warm and kind.

She stood the sandwich board up next to the table.

He looked it over carefully, then turned to her. "That's good work. It will certainly make people stop and read it. Where did you learn to do this?"

"I've always wanted to draw and paint. I was accepted to take interior design at Hastings starting in the fall."

"So, you're going back to school in a couple of weeks?"

"No. I've decided not to pursue my career in design." Treacherous tears formed behind her eyelids.

"That's too bad. You're talented, and deserve a chance to continue your studies."

Seeing the empathy in his eyes, Sarah had a feeling that he would be the kind of man who would help someone if they needed it.

He tapped the table. "Would you be willing to do this board every day?"

"Yes. Of course. I'd love it. Can I get a few more pieces of colored chalk? And maybe we could put paper copies of the lunch menu into a box at the bottom of the board."

"You think that would entice people in?"

"I think the tourists would like to compare menus, and what better way than to pick up a single sheet of paper with a listing of the lunch dishes?"

"Sarah Maddison, I like how you think."

His smile made her feel so appreciated. "You're okay if I do it? Can I do something else as well?"

He looked startled. "Like what?"

Had she spoken too soon? What if all the local paintings belonged to his friends, or worse, they were his paintings? She squirmed just a little in her chair. "I'd like to rearrange the art work in the restaurant, create a collage of paintings, maybe even prepare a special wall that showcases local artists." She saw his smile fade. "You don't like that idea? Sorry I didn't mean to push in where I don't belong."

"You didn't. To tell you the truth I've been wanting to do something with the paintings scattered all around the dining room, but didn't want to upset local patrons by changing things. Some patrons insist on sitting in the booth where their family member or friend's painting is displayed." He winced. "You see my problem, don't you?"

"I do. Let me think about it. I'll sketch something up at home tonight and see what you think. Would that work?"

"It certainly would." With that he went down the back hall to the kitchen, leaving Sarah feeling special and important. She was humming when she gathered her things and headed to the phone booth outside the restaurant.

CHAPTER ELEVEN

*P*utting change in the slot, she dialed her mom's number at work. "Mom, it's me. I just finished my first shift at the restaurant. I like it. I know I can do it, and everyone is so helpful."

"Oh, Sarah, it's so good to hear your voice. I miss you, honey. Your dad and I were going to call you tonight. Is there anything wrong? You're not sick are you?"

"No. No. I'm good."

"Did you meet anyone, make any friends?"

"The owner's really nice, and I'm working with a woman who is teaching me how to be a waitress."

"That's good. I'm so pleased."

"Mom, has anyone called for me?"

"You mean, Kevan?" There was a pause on the phone. "I hate to tell you this, honey, but Kevan hasn't called anyone that I know of other than his family. I've asked around trying to find out what is going on with him. One of the people in marketing who is in touch with the office in Ireland says Kevan is not coming back for at least a year."

"What!" Sarah cried out. "That can't be true. People are just gossiping."

"I don't know anything at this point. Each day I wait to hear if anyone knows anything concrete about when he's coming back home."

Filled with longing, Sarah steadied herself against the wall of the phone booth, her hands shaking. "What am I going to do, Mom?"

"You're going to take care of yourself, stay healthy. You're going to make an appointment with a doctor for a check-up. Your aunt will know the name of a good physician," she said gently but firmly.

"I will as soon as I can." Sarah closed her eyes, remembering the look on Kevan's face the last time she'd seen him; feeling his arms around her that day in the gymnasium. It seemed like a lifetime ago.

"You think I'm wrong about all this, that your dad and I are giving you bad advice. Why don't you talk to a doctor, see what they have to say?"

"I will, Mom." She gave a long sigh. "Right now, I need to get back to Elsie and Fred. They've been so kind."

"They've been really good to you, haven't they?"

"Yes."

"We'll call this evening, honey. You go home and get off your feet. Standing all day is really hard on your circulation, especially now."

After a few more bits of advice on diet and exercise while expecting, her mother rang off.

Hearing what her mother said made calling the McElroy house even more urgent.

She dialed the number she'd memorized in the days that followed Kevan's disappearance from her life. It rang four times. She was about to hang up when a woman answered. "It's Sarah Maddison. I need to speak to Julia."

"She's not available." The voice was crisp, cold and to the point.

"Can you give her a message for me?"

The line was so quiet Sarah feared that whoever had answered had hung up or put the phone down. "Why are you calling here?" the woman said.

"I need to speak to Kevan."

"What business do you have with my son?"

Her breath caught in her throat. "I... He's my boyfriend. He said he'd get in touch with me."

"Kevan is your boyfriend?" The steel-cold tone in the woman's voice shook her resolve.

"Yes."

"Let me be very clear, Miss Maddison. Kevan will not be in touch with you. He has a life that doesn't include you. Do I make myself clear?"

She gasped at the harsh words. "I only want to speak with him. I have something to tell him that can't wait."

"You have nothing to tell my son. Good day." The phone clicked in her ear.

Feeling dizzy, her stomach reeling, she leaned against the booth. "It can't be true!" she cried out.

"What can't be true?" a gentle male voice said.

She turned to see Benjamin Patterson standing behind her. *How much of that awful conversation had he heard?*

"Ah... It's just something that happened. Nothing really, I guess." She ducked her head and wiped her cheeks again, before glancing his way. His expression was one of concern, making her wish she could share with him what was going on in her life. But that was a useless idea. What was wrong in her life, no one could fix.

"It sounded pretty serious to me. You look really worried. You're staying with your aunt and uncle, right?"

"Yes." She sniffed.

"Can they help you with whatever is going on?" he asked.

"I don't know..."

"I'm sure they'd be willing to try. Why don't I drive you home?" he asked, pointing to the huge half-ton parked at the curb.

She needed to be alone, to work out what she could do after hearing Mrs. McElroy's words. "I'm okay. I'll walk home from here."

He stood there, not moving, simply watching her with a kind look in his eyes. "I saw the sandwich board you did for tomorrow's lunch specials. The staff think it's great and so do I."

His words pleased her, despite the sinking feeling in her tummy. "Thank you. I needed to hear that." She took a deep, sustaining breath. "It wasn't difficult at all. I loved doing it. I'll do it every day if you like," she said, realizing how eager she must sound to his ears. Being eager wasn't exactly cool, but at this moment she really didn't care.

He cocked his hands on his hips, his gaze assessing. "Why don't we look at my offer to drive you home this way? I'm going to drive my interior decorator home so she can come up with ideas for my restaurant. Wouldn't want anything to happen to the one person who might be able to help me out of my decorating disaster, would we?"

"No. We can't have that," she said, realizing that this was someone she could get to like...a lot.

"Then come on. We'll get you home so you can do your magic." He walked beside her toward his truck, and it felt so good, so natural. She looked up into his face, and noted with surprise and pleasure that he was smiling down at her.

WHEN HE'D FOUND Sarah at the phone booth, he knew she was upset about a call she'd made. It was none of his business, but after how well she did today, he wanted her to remain part of the staff – she fit in so easily. If her first day was any indication she was a good worker and enthusiastic – two essential traits in the restaurant business; she would work out well.

And the way she walked beside him companionably, not making what he considered to be nuisance conversation, appealed to him. He enjoyed being with her very much.

In fact, the easy way they were with each other, the sense of companionship made Benjamin feel good, the best he'd felt in a long time. There was something about this woman that intrigued him. Although she was young, she was also very capable and quick to offer her help when needed. He had spoken with Leslie Anne, and she had nothing but praise for Sarah. "Leslie Anne tells me that for someone who never waited tables before, you caught on fast."

"Thank you. I have to admit that I'm pretty tired, but I really enjoyed it. So many of the patrons are repeat customers, and they all know Leslie Anne."

"We've built our business on repeat customers. The tourists are great customers as well, but they're only around part of the year. The rest of the year we depend on locals." He was acutely aware of how much he wanted to keep this conversation going. Yet he knew so little about her, other than she had moved there from some-where near Boston. "Did you have a favorite restaurant back where you lived?"

Standing next to the passenger door of his truck, she hesitated for a moment. "I guess that would be the Sage and Thyme, a restaurant about two blocks from my house. It serves all sorts of soups and sandwiches – all homemade."

"I'll have to try it sometime. I make a point of eating at locally owned restaurants whenever I can. Helps me learn about the competition." *Why was he talking business, when all he really wanted to do was go for a walk with her, sit on a park bench, anything to spend time with her?*

Reluctantly he opened the truck door for her. "But let's not talk business anymore today." He watched her get into the truck and noted that she did it with complete ease, something most others found awkward. Going around to his side of the truck, he got in and started the engine. "Have you been in Bar Harbor before? I mean have you seen the town, where the shops are that you might need?" He sighed, feeling like a teenager on his first date.

"No. I haven't. So far everything I need has been provided by my aunt."

"Then, why don't I drive you around the downtown area? That way you'll have some idea where to go if you need something," he said, pleased to have an excuse to spend a little time with her.

"That's really kind of you," she said, smiling at him in a way that made him feel appreciated.

They drove around the downtown as he pointed out all the shops, the local pharmacy, the hardware store.

"I doubt I'll need to go there. Uncle Fred excels in the handyman department," she said, chuckling as she leaned forward to rest her hand on the edge of the window.

"You have a great laugh," he said, feeling so at ease with her.

She turned to him, a look of pleasure fading to longing, and suddenly he wanted to make her smile again. "Okay. Enough of the boring town sites. Let's go wild and drive up into Acadia National Park."

"I'd like that," she said, her expression once again happy. He decided in that moment he would make her smile whenever he got the chance.

They reached the park, and drove up to a look off area. "What do you think of this?" he asked, stopping the truck so they could take in the view. "I never tire of this sight," he said.

"It's beautiful," she said, a sigh escaping her lips. "Can we get out?"

"Sure." He jumped out, went to her door, and opened it. "This is where my mom and I used to have picnics when I was a kid, when Dad was busy with the restaurant," he added, realizing he'd never told any of his girlfriends about this place and what it meant to him.

She walked to the front of the truck, looking out over the wide expanse of forest to the ocean in the distance. "I've never seen anything like this in my life," she said, looking up into his face, her lips parted, her blonde hair spread out around her shoulders.

She is so beautiful....

The scent of something floral wafted around him as he stood beside her. "I grew up here, and yet I never tire of coming back to this spot, just to take in the view."

"Thank you for this," she said, her voice so low and quiet he had to duck his head to catch her words.

"You're welcome. If you'd like I can take you to see the sites around Bar Harbor when you have a day off and want to go with me... I mean if you'd like to go with me." Heaven help him. He sounded like a school boy, not a grown man.

She looked at him, seeming to study him before she answered. "Please don't put yourself out for me. I'm sure my uncle and aunt will take me to see places around here," she said, the look in her eyes one of indecision.

He felt a little foolish standing there, waiting for a woman he hardly knew to take him up on his offer. "I didn't mean to impose on you. Yes. I'm sure your aunt and uncle will take you around to see the area."

"No. Really. I would be happy to have you show me around the area," she said, as if she'd made her mind up about something.

"Then, let's get you home, and later we can decide when I'll give you your first tour. Sound good?"

"Absolutely." There was that smile again. That irresistible smile.

CHAPTER TWELVE

Standing in such a beautiful place, with a man she barely knew, Sarah had only one thought: She had never met anyone quite like Benjamin. Of course, not having dated a lot in high school probably explained her lack of experience with men. Yet, she felt so much better being around him.

It had been nice to simply be around someone kind and caring like Benjamin, someone who had no real place in her life, other than as her boss. During the drive home she watched him out of the corner of her eye, curious about what he must be thinking. He seemed so kind and interested in her. Flattered by his attention she wondered what sort of woman would appeal to a man as successful as Benjamin.

She spotted her uncle at the mail box as Benjamin pulled into the driveway. Fred waved and came over to the truck.

"Thanks for bringing our girl home, Benjamin. We're waiting to hear about her day."

"Hope she gives us all a passing grade," he said.

"I will," Sarah said as she climbed out of the truck. "Thank you for the ride. I'll see you tomorrow."

"As for the sketches, take your time. I'd rather you came up with something really great than feeling you have to rush them." He nodded to her as he eased the truck out of the driveway.

Her uncle squeezed her shoulders. "Elsie and I have been waiting to hear all about your day. Getting a drive home with the boss is a really good sign," he said as he followed her up the steps to the front door.

"Was everything okay today?" Elsie asked the minute Sarah got into the kitchen.

"Everything was fine. I really like the job," she said, remembering the disastrous moments on the phone with Mrs. McElroy.

"I knew you would. While I get dinner organized I want you to tell me all about it."

Patches stretched and came out from under one of the kitchen chairs. Giving her his wide-eyed cat look, he leapt up into her lap. She talked cat talk for a few minutes while she thought about what she could do now that there was no hope that anyone at the McElroy house was willing to help her contact Kevan. She told her aunt about her workday, while her mind stayed with Kevan and the awful phone call she'd had with Mrs. McElroy.

"Aunt Elsie, I can't seem to find anything out from Kevan's family about where he is. Mom says that I need to forget about him, and concentrate on my life here and staying healthy for my baby's sake. But I love Kevan, and I need to know where he is, and how he's making out. There's no way he wouldn't be in touch with me, but since I've moved, and Mom says he hasn't called home, I don't know what to do."

"Sarah, honey, there is something you need to understand. People like the McElroy family have every form of communication available to them. Kevan could be in touch with his family, or your family or your friends, if he wanted to. I hate to be cruel but you need to accept the fact that it has been months since you saw him last. And in all that time you haven't heard a word from him, have you?"

She sighed, her heart heavy with defeat. "No. I haven't. But I can't give up trying. Something must have happened to him."

Her aunt sat down at the table next to Sarah. "Don't spend any more time waiting for him. You need to think about getting to see a doctor here, and enjoying your job before you're asked to leave because of your condition."

"Why would I be asked to leave?" she asked, surprised.

"Sarah, as you get bigger and more awkward working around tables, carrying trays, you won't be able to continue. And you may not feel well enough. You never know. But spending all your mental and emotional energy, on finding a man who doesn't seem to want to be found, won't help you or your pregnancy. That's why you need to see a doctor and get your life organized."

Sarah stared at her aunt. "What do you mean?"

"I mean that the best hope you have of finding good parents for your baby will be through a doctor who has cared for you during your pregnancy and knows of a childless couple looking for a baby. That's the reality. Not all this wishing and hoping for someone who has moved on."

CHAPTER THIRTEEN

The next week, and after another night of restless sleep, Sarah awoke from a bad dream in which she'd seen Kevan, had called out to him, and he'd kept walking away from her. Barely awake, she felt suddenly nauseated and nearly didn't make it to the bathroom before she was sick to her stomach. Feeling miserable, she went downstairs, made herself a piece of dry toast to ease her stomach – something her mother had suggested on the phone the other day. She'd finally gotten used to starting her days this way, but it wasn't easy, and the jeans she'd worn yesterday to help her uncle plant a rose bush had felt tight.

The clock on the kitchen stove said 5:00, too early to go to work, and too late to go back to bed. As Patches jumped up on her lap, she held him close, feeling the gentle thumping of his heart under her finger tips.

"Patches, Kevan is coming back, isn't he?" she whispered into the cat's fur. Patches stretched up toward her face, and nudged her cheek. "I'm so glad I have you. We see life the same way, don't we?"

Patches reached up and swatted her chin gently, his furry paw such a soothing touch. They sat together as the sky began to lighten. After a few minutes, the cat jumped down and scurried over to the pile of pencils, erasers and sharpeners sprawled across the desk in the corner of the kitchen.

"You want me to get to work on my drawings for Benjamin, don't you?" she said, smiling at the ease with which she had slipped into cat talk this morning.

Feeling more upbeat she gathered her art supplies and settled herself on the sofa in the living room. With Patches perched beside her she began sketching, and before long she had several ideas she could show her boss. Pleased with herself, she went to the kitchen and made coffee, taking a cup upstairs with her as she got ready for work.

She put on her clean uniform, and marveled again at how perfect the color was, highlighting her sun-streaked hair. She felt so lucky in so many ways. She'd found a job she liked.

Benjamin was being so kind, a true friend. And Leslie Anne and she were becoming friends. Not in the same way she and Cindy were friends, but in a way that was both pleasant and rewarding. Leslie Anne had recommended a hair stylist who had done a really nice cut, making her hair bounce around her shoulders. She had settled in with her aunt and uncle without disrupting their lives too much, and heard from her parents every weekend.

Gazing at herself in the mirror she noted that the uniform fit well across her waist and the top was comfortable when she wind-milled her arms in front of the mirror. It was important that it be loose enough for her to move easily, as carrying trays and removing plates required much more dexterity than she'd realized. She had to admit that with only a few days on the job she had learned a lot.

Gathering her purse and jacket, she headed downstairs.

"You're not leaving without breakfast, are you?" her aunt asked, tightening the belt of her robe and glancing around the sun-drenched kitchen as Sarah entered.

"I was up earlier and had a bite to eat."

Elsie hesitated for a moment. "Can I say something?"

Sarah saw the worried expression on her aunt's face. "Sure."

"This isn't easy for me to say. I talked with your Mom yesterday. She overheard someone in her office talking about Kevan and his job in Ireland. It seems that the business over there is growing faster than in Boston, and they are hiring more people, and if this means that Kevan has an even bigger commitment to his job over there…"

"Why didn't Mom tell me this herself?" Sarah asked.

Elsie took Sarah's hand in hers. "She's worried about you. We all love you and want you to be happy. You need to remember that your family are the ones who are here for you. Not Kevan…regardless of his reasons."

"And you agree with Mom that he's not coming back."

Elsie nodded her head slowly.

If what her mother overheard was true, Kevan had made a life for himself in Ireland, one she had no role in. Trying to fight off the rising panic, she said, "I need to get to work."

"Do you want a drive? I can get dressed and take you."

She needed time to sort through her feelings. "No. I like the walk. I need to think about what you said." She kissed her aunt's cheek, taking in her sweet lavender scent. "I'll be home for supper." Grabbing her pencil sketches she headed out the front door and along the walkway to the street.

FOUR HOURS LATER, she hadn't had a break. The walk into work had been filled with thoughts of Kevan and her disbelief that he would betray her this way. Thankfully, she'd been too busy since then to worry.

When she'd arrived at the restaurant she'd hoped to distract herself by finding a few minutes to show Benjamin what she'd done by reworking the local artists' paintings, but the restaurant was half full minutes after they opened. Still, she'd enjoyed the morning and the people she met. They were all so kind and generous.

"You'd better grab a bite of lunch before things go crazy again," Leslie Anne said, looking closely at Sarah. "In fact, your color isn't very good. Are you feeling okay?"

Sarah couldn't admit to how queasy she felt. It would mean she'd have to explain.

"I'm starving. I'll eat quickly and get back so you can go eat," she said, heading to the back of the restaurant. In the kitchen the cook made her a grilled cheese sandwich and ladled up a steaming bowl of chicken soup. The smell intensified her hunger. Aware that she needed to get back to help Leslie Anne she ate quickly. She had just finished her sandwich when Benjamin came to the table and sat down across from her.

"Busy morning," he said, watching her wipe her lips with a napkin.

Sitting across from Benjamin felt good. "Yes. So many people come in here and behave as if it's their second home." She gathered her dishes and took them to the dish return area before coming back to sit down for a few minutes. "I finished the sketches I promised."

"That's great. Can I see them?"

"They're in my locker. I can get them now if you like, Mr. Patterson."

"It's Benjamin to my friends, and thank you. I'd really like to see what you came up with."

"I'll be right back," she said, heading for the back corridor of the restaurant. When she returned, she unfolded the diagrams to show him what she'd done.

"You have a large wall at the front entrance, just to the right of the hostess station. If that wall were lit with small spot lights, and the wall was painted a soft gold tone, I could put together a collage of paintings with each artist mentioned with their painting. Leslie

Anne said the artists want to sell these painting, and if their work were more centrally located more people would see what they've done. I also thought that we could move a long, narrow table in front of the wall of paintings with the business cards of each of the artists. That way anyone looking to buy a painting would be able to contact the artist."

"And how do I answer the people who want to sit next to a particular painting?"

"You tell them that their work will be on display for the entire restaurant clientele to view."

"That's brilliant." He smiled at her. "I wasn't sure what you'd come up with but that will work very well." He gave her an assessing glance. "Mary, my full-time hostess on the reservation desk, just told me she's leaving to get married and move to Portland. I'd like to offer you the job, on condition that you organize what you just described and that you promote the art work a little bit while clients wait for their tables. What do you think?"

She fingered the gold locket resting along the curve of her neck, feeling her past slipping ever so gently aside. A moment of guilt touched her, quickly followed by the reality before her. Her boss thought she had done something really special for his restaurant, and until she heard from Kevan, this was her life. "I...I'd love that. It would give me a chance to do a little interior design in a space where so many people come to relax and enjoy themselves." She forced her mind away from all the interesting things her classmates at Hastings would be doing this fall without her. "Thank you for this opportunity."

His eyes met hers: He toyed with the pen he held in his powerful hands, slowly turning it over and over.

"Would you like to go sailing with me sometime?" he asked.

"Sailing? You want *me* to go sailing with *you*?" she asked, as feelings of excitement flitted through her mind. She had never been on a sailboat, and now she would have the opportunity. "I...I...

don't know," she said, feeling a little reckless for the first time in her life.

BENJAMIN FELT a sudden jab of misgiving. *What was he doing?* He mentioned that he'd take her around to see the area, but getting her on his sailboat... The confined space below deck... The narrow cockpit area where they couldn't help but touch each other regardless of how innocent.

This was hardly the way to behave around a member of his staff, and he certainly didn't need to create any difficult work situations. "That... Sorry. I had no business asking you to go sailing with me."

"Not a problem... Not at all." She touched the locket again, this time lifting it gently. "You took me by surprise. No one has ever asked me to go sailing, or anything like that. I would really love to go out on your boat."

Relief whistled through him at her enthusiastic response, at the soft curve of her lips that made him wonder what it would be like to once again have a woman in his life. "Then it's a date. The day after tomorrow the weather is supposed to be sunny and hot. Why don't we go after your shift finishes? I'll get the cook to pack a picnic for us. I'll drive you home so you can change first."

Her smile of acceptance, so warm and open, eased the tension in his shoulders. How could a smile do that? He didn't know.

As his eyes met hers he was reminded of how hard he worked, how little fun he had in his life, and how determined he was to change all that if he could. He deserved to spend a summer day with a beautiful young woman, a woman who could light his life with her smile.

. . .

A LITTLE LATER, while they were standing at the order counter, Leslie Anne turned to her and gave her a big smile. "Spill it, now," she said.

"Spill what?"

"Why are you looking so happy? In fact, you're looking the happiest I've ever seen you."

"Benjamin liked my drawings."

"I think he likes more than that." Leslie Anne lifted one brow in question. "I've seen the way he looks at you. He doesn't look at any of the rest of us that way."

Sarah wanted to confide in someone about the sailing trip, but worried that people would talk if they knew, and people talking about her would mean they'd talk even more when they found out she was pregnant. "He's just being kind."

Leslie Anne hugged her. "I'll let it go for now. Not because I'm finished with you on this subject, but because I am going to die of hunger if I don't get to eat."

Sarah didn't have any more time to think about the sailing trip as she made her way to the tables to check on how people were doing. When Leslie Anne returned they worked non-stop until near the end of the shift.

They were folding napkins when Leslie Anne asked, "Do you have a boyfriend?"

"Yes. I mean...my boyfriend went to Ireland."

"Do you talk to him? Write letters? How do you stay in touch?"

Sarah wasn't sure how to explain her situation. "It's difficult, but..."

"I don't have anyone in my life, and right now I don't want anyone. I have Sammy to take care of, and he's a busy four-year-old."

Sarah had heard Leslie Anne talk about her son, but didn't know the details of her life, and had never felt it her place to ask. "Who takes care of him when you're working?"

"My mom some of the time, when she isn't working at the fish-packing plant. Otherwise I have a neighbor who keeps kids, and I take him there."

"What's it like? Working and looking after your little boy?"

"Hard at times, but I wouldn't have it any other way. I love my boy. And with his dad gone, I'm all he has – me and my family." She turned to Sarah, pride evident in her expression. "Gregory was killed in a fishing accident. We had only been married two years and were expecting Sammy when he died."

Sarah put her arms around her friend. "I'm sorry. That must have been horrible."

"It was. If it hadn't been for Mom and Dad I don't know what I would have done. And working here, being busy and able to earn money to look after my son has helped me get over Gregory's death." She sniffed and smiled. "Don't get me going or I will simply stand here and cry."

"I had no idea," Sarah said, feeling closer to Leslie Anne after hearing about her life.

"I don't advertise. Everyone in town knows what happened. They've all been really kind to me."

Sarah had so many questions she wanted to ask Leslie Anne, yet she couldn't. She had to keep her situation to herself, at least until she saw the doctor tomorrow.

CHAPTER FOURTEEN

*T*he next day Sarah went to Dr. Harding's office to be told she was healthy and that her pregnancy was moving along with no noted complications or issues. Knowing Aunt Elsie and her mother were determined that she give her baby up for adoption, she asked the doctor about what would be involved, explaining her family's concerns. Dr. Harding was very kind, saying that for now her health and her baby's health was all she needed to be concerned about.

If Sarah should decide to put her baby up for adoption, they could talk about it when she was in the later months of her pregnancy. The doctor examined her, ordered blood work and gave her another appointment.

Once all of the procedures were completed, Dr. Harding sat down in front of her. "I believe you are about fourteen weeks along. Is the father of your baby involved in this pregnancy with you?"

"No. He's in Ireland."

"Does he know?" the doctor asked kindly.

"Not yet."

"Do you intend to tell him?"

"If I can find him," Sarah said.

Dr. Harding leaned forward in her chair again, her expression kind and thoughtful. "I hope you find him, if that's what you want."

"I do."

She liked this woman who seemed so confident, so certain, so unlike how she had been feeling all these weeks. "Thank you." She left the office feeling that she had an ally in all this. A woman who understood what she was feeling.

She was walking up the street to the restaurant when Leslie Anne caught up with her.

"Hold up, Sarah."

"Hi Leslie Anne, how's it going?"

"Good. Really good. I'm glad we have a chance to talk before our shift. Why didn't you tell me that you were invited out on the boss's sailboat."

"How did you find out?"

Leslie Anne gave a knowing smile. "He ordered Bruce, the short order cook, to make up a picnic basket, and Bruce overheard him telling someone on the phone that he wanted the tanks topped up with fuel because he was taking the boat out."

"Has Bruce told everyone at the restaurant?" Sarah asked, self-conscious at the thought that the people she worked with knew she had a date with the boss.

Leslie Anne nodded her head, giving a low, throaty chuckle. "News like that travels like wildfire. Everyone wants to know what the boss is doing with his free time. Not that he has much, but all that same... Besides this isn't the 'burbs' of Boston. This is Bar Harbor, and don't you forget it."

"I'll try not to," she said.

"You seem down. What's the matter?"

She looked at Leslie Anne. She needed to confide in someone, to let go of the ache building inside her, to have someone she could trust with what she was feeling. Someone who would listen. "Leslie

Anne, can I tell you something? It's personal and I don't want anyone else to know, at least not right away."

"Even if I wanted to tell someone something, where would I find the time with Sammy *and* a full-time job?" she teased.

What if she lost her job when Benjamin found out she was pregnant? Surely, he wouldn't do that... "You have to promise me that you won't talk to anyone about this."

"I promise."

Sarah swallowed as anxiety spun a web in her mind, making her feel tense and uncertain. "I'm...I'm expecting a baby."

"You're *what*?" Leslie Anne stopped in the middle of the sidewalk, grabbed her arm. "I thought...I thought you were here until you went back home to go to school. That's what I heard... That's not true?"

"No. I'm here to have my baby. Kevan's and my baby."

"Where is this Kevan person?"

Sarah went on to explain her dilemma.

"Oh, Sarah, I'm so sorry. I can't imagine what you must be feeling about all that."

"I want to keep this baby. I mean, I believe Kevan will get in touch with me while he's in Ireland. He has to. And I will not decide about my baby until I talk to him," she said stubbornly.

Leslie Anne's smile was gentle. "How long has he been gone?"

"Almost three months." She felt the tears start behind her eyes and looked away.

Leslie Anne took her hand. "You're in a bad spot. You need to decide what you are going to do. Either you insist on finding Kevan, or you make plans to have this baby on your own."

"I know." She went on to explain what Kevan's father had threatened to do if anyone pressured him about his son's life and plans.

"So, contacting him has consequences for your parents. That is just awful."

"My mom and aunt think that Kevan's run off on me."

"What if he has?"

"He wouldn't do that to me, and if he knew about our baby he would be here. I know he would." She covered her face with her hands to ward off the awful thought that maybe Kevan had left her. She had strenuously tried to block any thought like that, but the longer she waited to hear from him, the more unsure she became. "My aunt and uncle have given me a place to live until I have the baby, and they expect me to put my baby up for adoption. Leslie Anne, I can't do that."

"I couldn't either. When Gregory died and I was alone there were times when I thought that maybe I couldn't manage a baby and a job. But I couldn't imagine my life without him."

"That's how I feel," Sarah said, relieved to hear that her friend agreed with her.

"Then, we need to get to work on a plan."

CHAPTER FIFTEEN

When they got to the restaurant, Benjamin was at the reservation desk, his head bent close to the hostess. There was something so appealing about him, so safe and protective in the way he stood there. He reminded her a little of her dad as well as Kevan in the way he listened to what the woman was saying.

When he spotted her, he came out from behind the desk, touching her elbow as he guided her to a quiet corner near the bar. "I needed to catch you before you start your shift. There's been a change of plans. I want you to get started on the collage of paintings, and I'd like you to come with me to the paint store to find the color you think will work."

"Now?" she asked.

"You don't want to?" he asked, a crestfallen look on his face. A look she would never have associated with him.

"I'd like to, if I'm not needed here."

"They can spare you for a couple of hours."

"Okay."

"Then, let's go." He followed her out to the rear parking lot to his truck.

A few minutes later she was standing in front of a wall of paint samples. She moved to the gold/yellow tones, her fingers moving over the samples, picking out one, then another, then putting one back. She was so absorbed in what she was doing she didn't see how close Benjamin was standing to her until they accidentally bumped into each other.

"WHOOPS! Didn't mean to get in the way of my interior decorator and her search for the perfect color," he said, stepping back out of Sarah's way. He liked the way she worked with such concentration, giving him an opportunity to watch her without being obvious.

And what he saw he liked – and he liked her more each time he was around her. No one held his attention like Sarah Maddison did. He just plain liked being with this woman, from the way she moved, to the look in her eyes when their eyes met, to the unfathomable sense that this woman would always do the best she could and care for those she loved.

"Have you been out in a sailboat before?" *What a dumb question! She already told me she hadn't.*

She turned those incredible eyes on him, causing him to suck in his stomach. *When was the last time he worried about whether or not his stomach needed to be sucked in? How was it that a young woman, ten years his junior, could make him feel like a crazy teenager?*

"I've never been in one in my life," she said, her hand poised over a collection of paint chips that didn't look like they'd go with anything in his restaurant. "And for heaven's sake, don't let me drive the boat. I have no sense of direction," she said.

He laughed. "I'm guessing you'll need a bit of instruction on how to handle a boat." He nodded at the collection of paint samples in her hand. "Which paint color are we buying?" he asked.

"None of them for now. I'm taking all of the samples I've picked out back to the restaurant. Then I will try them against the space we're talking about, and pick two. Then we will come back here and get two small sample cans. I will paint part of the wall with each of them, and see which color works best. When is the electrician coming to change the lighting? And when can we go looking for the table we need?"

"The electrician will be there tomorrow." He felt secretly pleased that she included him when she put together the materials she needed. "That reminds me: He asked that you drop by and pick out the three light fixtures for the wall."

"Great." She looked so happy as she walked past him. "Let's go."

He followed her as she wove through the various displays of the hardware store, her body swaying as she moved. He wondered to himself what it would be like to touch her, to feel her body close to his…

Get a grip! A woman as pretty as Sarah would have a boyfriend. He caught up to her at the door, pulling it open for her. "I can see you enjoy this sort of thing. Did you say you had applied to take an interior design course?"

She glanced up at him, a small furrow forming between her perfectly round eyes. "I did. But I decided to come here."

"When your uncle first asked me to give you a job, he didn't say how long you'd be staying. Do you know yet?" he asked, leading the way across the parking lot to his truck.

"I'll be here at least until Christmas. Beyond that I'm not sure."

"Sounds great." He couldn't keep the delight from his voice. "Christmas in Bar Harbor is beautiful – the lights on the water, the store windows all decorated. We have a huge Christmas market down along the waterfront. You'll love it. Maybe you'll want to put something in the Christmas market. I can check into getting you a table if you'd like."

"That would be wonderful. I would love to put some of my paintings in. I could even paint a couple of new scenes of the harbor, the restaurant as well…"

Getting into the truck, she settled her hands in her lap and didn't look his way. He started the engine and still she didn't look at him. *What was going on behind those beautiful eyes?*

"Would you like to stop for lunch before we go to look at lights?"

"No. It's okay. Let's finish up and then I can get back to work," she said.

When they went to the lighting store Sarah barely spoke to him. He was paying for the three light fixtures when he decided to see if he could figure out what was going on with her. "Do you like Christmas?"

She brightened. "I love it. The lights. The way everyone is out shopping, going to visit Santa. And I love trimming the tree. I made all the ornaments on our Christmas tree at home."

He wanted to see her smile. "Would you be willing to decorate the restaurant for Christmas?"

She turned to him, her eyes alight. "I would love that. I assume you have a ton of decorations already. I'll go through them, organize the colors." She rubbed her hands together. "This is great. Thank you."

"I'll leave it in your capable hands."

A look of concern came over her face. "You won't expect me to get up on a ladder, will you?"

"Do ladders frighten you?"

"No. It's just that…" She turned away and once again he had the feeling she was hiding something. Something very important in her life.

CHAPTER SIXTEEN

*L*ater that evening as Sarah settled in for another evening of hoping that Kevan would call, she wondered if maybe her family was right. Kevan wasn't coming back. Treacherous thoughts.

All along she believed that he'd contact her as soon as he could, yet with each passing day she resigned herself to the very real possibility that she might not hear from Kevan ever again.

She tried not to think about what it would mean to her if he wasn't coming back. She'd kept working at her job, doing everything she could to stay positive, living with the belief that he would find her, and they would begin to plan for their baby.

Yet, despite her need to see Kevan, she had to admit that for the first time in a very long time she really enjoyed herself during the time she spent with Benjamin. At first, she believed he was simply a distraction, but when she got home she couldn't stop the feelings of happiness being with him had created. What she liked most about their time together today was that he believed in her, trusted her to complete the project.

When she and Benjamin got back to the restaurant she went to work on the wall she planned to decorate, and very quickly decided on the color of paint she needed. She told Benjamin and he went to the hardware store for the two cans of sample paint she needed. During their time at the paint store and afterward he didn't try to influence her choices, or offer ideas. He let her do what she needed to do, and she was grateful.

Tomorrow was going to be such a wonderful day. Benjamin had hired the painter to work early in the morning before the customers came in, and she'd be able to see how it looked before they went out on his sailboat. When she'd told Elsie and Fred about going out in the sailboat they'd been delighted for her – a little too excited.

Did they think this was a real date? Was it a real date? Benjamin had asked her to go with him in a very casual way, and she'd assumed he simply wanted to show her around a bit as he'd done one other day. *But was that all it really was?*

She was still thinking about it when she fell asleep.

THE NEXT MORNING shone with bright sunlight and a scrubbed blue sky. She was going sailing today. A new experience that she looked forward to. For the first time in weeks, she didn't wake up feeling nauseated, for which she was very thankful. Pulling on her blue jeans she noted that they were a bit snug. Turning sideways to the mirror she checked her side view. A very tiny bump showed, or maybe it was her imagination.

Aunt Elsie's call from the kitchen broke into her reverie. "I'm coming. I'm just about ready," she said, grabbing her wind breaker, a scarf and pulling on her sneakers.

When she reached the kitchen, she fed Patches, ran her fingers through his fur, for which he offered up a chorus of purring sounds. "Hey, handsome, you like that, don't you?" He answered by ducking his head further into his food bowl.

"When will you be back?" her aunt asked.

"I don't have the foggiest idea," she said.

"Are you dressed warm enough?"

"Well, this is all I have to wear so it will have to do."

"That reminds me, we're going to have to go out and get you a couple maternity tops pretty soon," her aunt said as she passed Sarah a cup of coffee. "I think we should go to Bangor to do the shopping for you. You're going to need pants too."

"Aunt Elsie, we aren't going to be able to hide me much longer."

"I know, dear, I only hope you're ready for what will happen when people find out you're expecting a baby."

"Nothing. People will know, that's all."

"What about people like Benjamin? He's your boss. What will he say when you start showing up at work with your top or your pants too tight. I think you should tell him. He might be able to give you a job other than as a waitress."

"He has. I'm decorating the restaurant and going to be the new hostess, at least for now," she said, feeling defensive. *Why did she always feel like some sort of odd creature?* Lots of people had babies. *Did they all hide out somewhere until their babies were born?*

"That's wonderful. Do you think he suspects something?"

She hadn't thought about it, but if he did... "No. He is not that kind of person." She wouldn't tell her aunt she'd confided in Leslie Anne. They had met twice for coffee to talk about how Sarah would be able to manage, once the baby was born.

She glanced at the clock. "Benjamin should be here any moment," she said and then heard the sound of a truck pulling into the driveway. "That's him now. I've got to go." She kissed her aunt's cheek, barely noting the lavender scent she'd grown accustomed to. "I'll see you when I get back."

"Have a good time."

. . .

BENJAMIN WAS JUST GETTING out of the truck when Sarah appeared at the door.

"All ready?" he asked, taking in her easy smile, the way the sun played with her hair. She was so beautiful, and she seemed so totally unaware of her beauty, making her even more alluring.

"Yes." She moved toward the truck, her hair flowing around her face, touching her cheeks, making him wish he could run his fingers through it.

Instead he opened the passenger door for her. "It turns out the painter isn't going to do the painting until later today or possibly not until tomorrow. So, I decided to take the day off. We'll go sailing, catch the outgoing tide and then come back to the restaurant. I have life vests on the boat."

"Will we need them?"

"The water may look lovely, but at this latitude, it's cold, and not great for swimming except in areas that are shallow and have a sandy beach. Do you swim?"

"Not well."

"Until you've gained a little time on the water I think it is important for you to wear a vest." *Did he sound pompous?* He dearly hoped not.

"Aye, Captain," she said, a teasing tone in her voice.

"Okay. We're off." Through the whole drive to the marina he had this urge to touch her, to feel her skin beneath his.

When they arrived, she helped him take blankets and the picnic basket down the floating dock, along one side to where the *Moon Stone* was moored. He stepped into the cockpit, put the picnic basket down and held out his hand to her. "Welcome aboard."

She took his hand, teetering just a bit as she climbed over the side to stand next to him. He couldn't help noticing that if the opportunity ever came, she would fit perfectly in his arms.

They stood there for a few minutes looking at each other. The boat, gently rocked by the wake of a passing boat, moved beneath them, bringing her tantalizingly close to him. Looking into her eyes, he felt as if they were somehow joined, connected. "Guess I'd better take the picnic hamper down below. Then we'll get ready to sail."

"Can I help?" she asked, her smile a little shaky.

"Yes. Come with me and I'll show you where the head is, and how to handle the refrigerator."

"Head?" she asked a quizzical look on her face.

"Bathroom?" He wanted to hug her. Instead he took the picnic hamper and went down below.

"Oh, I see. A nautical term for the bathroom on a boat," she said, following close behind him.

"You got it." He waited for her to come down the steps, then watched in amusement as she looked around, taking everything in for the first time.

"Do you sail often?" she asked, her eyes surveying the space one more time before coming to rest on him.

"I'm usually too busy." He stood almost toe-to-toe with her in the narrow space, and had to force his hands behind his back so as not to give in and simply take her in his arms.

She looked up into his face, as she slowly pulled a strand of hair off her cheek. "What do we do now?" she asked.

All he wanted to do was take her in his arms, and kiss her senseless. "I guess we go out on the deck and prepare to leave the harbor."

"Do you need me for that?"

"It'd be really great if you could undo the lines holding the boat to the cleats on the dock."

"Sure." She looked at him for a moment, with that cute little smile turning up the corners of her mouth, then turned and headed up the steps.

They worked together casting off the boat lines and getting the engine started. "I'm going to use the motor until we clear the harbor, then I'll put the sails up. You can sit right there." He pointed to a seat near the companionway. Reaching into the cupboard under the cockpit bench he pulled out a life vest. "Here. Put this on."

From the corner of his eye he watched her fasten the zipper and adjust the vest over her body. Doing his best to focus on anything other than her body, he edged the boat out into the space leading to the entrance of the harbor. The briny smell of the sea, the easy ebb and flow of the water around the boat as he angled out into the main channel, gave him a feeling of freedom he didn't get anywhere else in his busy life.

And today he had a beautiful woman with him, someone he admired and wanted to be around, if only to share something as simple as taking his boat out. "I hope you enjoy your day with me," he said, kicking himself for saying "me." *What was he thinking?* It sounded like he was looking for a cheesy compliment. *Way to go.*

As they rounded the breakwater the wind caught the boat, pushing it sideways. For a fleeting moment Sarah looked anxious, but recovered quickly. "I should have asked this before, but do you get seasick?"

"No. At least not that I know of." She hugged herself as she stared out under the boom.

He couldn't help but notice that she was chewing her lip. "You don't have to worry. This boat is safe, and we will turn back at any time you feel you're not comfortable."

"No. It's fine. This is going to be fun."

And it was. Once clear of the harbor, Benjamin raised the sails, feeling the strength of the wind as the sails filled. The sun glinted off the foresail rigging. The wind charged past them as the boat began to lean into the wind. Unable to resist any longer, he sat down next to her, his body forming a break from the wind.

"Would you like to take the tiller?" he asked, searching for any opportunity he could find to put his arms around her.

"Okay. I'll try." She slid closer to him, and following his instructions she took the tiller, holding the boat into the wind as if she'd done it before. He sat close, and took in the sight of her holding the boat on course, her expression eager and at the same time a little pensive.

"You're doing just fine," he said, offering her his support while enjoying every moment with her. "But why don't I put it on autopilot so I can point out some of the shoreline we might want to visit one of these days."

They talked about work, the sights to be seen along the shore, about her uncle and aunt, about her dream of someday having her own interior design business. They were huddled together talking, her breath warm on his cheeks.

"I really like this, the sailing I mean. I've never done anything like this in my life," she said, turning her face into his shoulder.

He couldn't take his eyes off her, couldn't let go of the feeling that if he kissed her she'd let him.

"I'm glad... So glad," he said, touching her face, letting his fingers play along her cheek bone, waiting for her to pull away. If she did he would not touch her again, and would move far enough away from her making sure that he wouldn't even touch her accidently.

With a shuddering sigh, Sarah settled into his arms. His heart hammered in his chest. Slowly, he kissed her, tasting the sweetness of her. He placed his hand on the back of her head, and eased his lips over hers, gently, with the pleasure of their kiss coursing through him.

His kiss, the tender pressure on her lips, the gentleness with which he held her, left her reeling.

FEELING the kind of she'd never experienced before, she put her arms around his neck and drew him to her.

He held her in his powerful arms as he looked into her eyes. "Sarah," he sighed, his blue eyes searching hers. "I want you—"

A horn blared a warning. Someone called out, "Starboard!"

Benjamin jumped away from her, grabbed the tiller and disconnected the autopilot as he swung away from the oncoming sailboat.

"Darn!" He waved to the crew on the other boat, before settling back down beside her.

"What happened?" she asked, feeling a little shaken, the taste of his lips lingering on hers.

"A little mix up about who had right of way," he said, his expression contrite.

She looked out over the roiling water, the sun glinting off the tiny caps of white. She'd never been this far out on the water in her life. Bewildered, she asked, "Are we okay?"

He turned to her, his expression one of concern. "We're fine. I'm going to attach a little awning over the cockpit while we have our lunch on deck."

"I'll help you."

"You can, but I'd rather you simply sat there while I get lunch ready."

"You are being so kind to me," she said, fighting to get her feelings under control. He'd kissed her and she'd liked it.

"Being kind to you is…what I do."

"And I appreciate everything you've done since I moved here. I was really worried in the beginning about how well we'd get along, but you've made me feel so welcome," she said, working the conversation back to something safe while she wondered if the kiss had meant to him what it meant to her.

"That's because I feel as if you and I have a connection, a way of seeing things. I'd like to see more of you, away from work, I mean." He played with the line resting on the edge of the deck, watching her.

She was feeling so mixed up right now…yet he seemed so calm.

He got up, went below and brought the picnic basket back, opened it and took out the sandwiches nestled on plates and wrapped with plastic wrap. He passed her one, and a soda, without saying a word.

Had she hurt him? She didn't mean to. Especially someone who had been so good to her. Removing the wrap, she took a bite of the sandwich. "This is good," she said, knowing that what she said was not what he wanted to hear.

"Look, Benjamin, I don't know what to say. You're my boss. You lead an entirely different life than I do. I'm new in town and I like you a lot." She was reminded of his kiss, and her cheeks flamed bright pink.

"Is that all?" he asked, looking out toward the horizon. "I enjoyed kissing you, but I don't know how you felt about it."

She touched her lips with a napkin, remembering the feel of his lips on hers and how much she wanted to feel his touch again. "It..." What could she say that wouldn't lead him to believe something that wasn't true? "I've never known someone like you."

"Someone like me? What does that mean?" He searched her face, his careful scrutiny making her breath come in tiny gasps.

She couldn't tell him how his kiss made her feel, how easily she could move back into his arms and stay there. She couldn't do it because she felt disloyal to Kevan. She had promised to love him forever, and it confused her that now she wanted another man to kiss her.

He looked out toward the horizon, his expression unreadable. "If you're already in a relationship, please say so."

"I...I'm just not sure if this is a good idea."

"You feel I'm too old for you?"

"No! I just think we should take it slow, remember that we work together and it might cause problems."

He turned to her, touching her hand where it rested on her knee. "You let me worry about that. In fact, let me do the worrying

91

for you whenever I can. I like you, Sarah. And the people I like, I want to look out for." He gave her a gentle hug. "And I can accept that you're not sure where we're going or what we're doing. I feel that way too."

His smile wrapped its warmth around her heart, lifting her spirits and making her feel that her life was about to change in a very nice way. "I enjoy being with you," she said, aware that her feelings for him had changed in the past hours. Being alone with him, his kiss, his confession that he'd look after her because he cared about her had changed everything she believed about their relationship.

He gave a long sigh, before letting her go. "Speaking of looking out for you. I think it might be time to head back. Your nose is a little pink. A touch of sunburn, maybe?"

She touched her nose and grinned at him. "I should have brought along some sunscreen."

He went below and brought up a tube of cream. "Here, put some of this on."

Something as simple as applying sunscreen felt like an intimate act between them, and she found herself enjoying the moment. She passed it back to him. "Thank you. If my nose starts to peel tomorrow, don't say anything."

"My lips are sealed," he said, reaching toward her, hesitating for a moment, then tousling her hair.

Happiness rippled through her—at the day, the moment of connection, but mostly at his touch and his caring. She needed both.

They finished their lunch in companionable silence, with the sun warming the air around them. When he turned the boat around to head back, she stood beside him, trying to learn as much as she could about the boat, but also to be near him.

When they returned to the marina, he turned to her, his body so close to her she could touch him.

"I'll drive you home," he said, tying the boat up to the dock. "Unless you need to run errands, or something..."

She touched her cheeks and felt the heat of them beneath her fingers. She wanted to stay with him, maybe go back to the restaurant. But he'd replaced her for her shift so that they could go sailing. To ask to go with him to work would be showing him that she wanted more time with him.

And what if he read more into her actions than she intended?

"No. I'd better get home and look after my sunburn." She walked ahead of him up the floating dock. "I'll see you tomorrow morning?"

"Absolutely."

Unease haunted her thoughts. She had been certain of what she was doing when she picked the colors, and arranged the layout of the photographs. But was she? "If you don't mind I'm going to come in early to work with the painter."

"You're not doubting yourself, are you?" he asked, a smile crinkling the skin around his eyes, the same eyes, that at times, seemed able to read her thoughts.

"Maybe. This is my first project, ever," she said, suddenly aware of how important it was to her that he approve of her work.

CHAPTER SEVENTEEN

*L*ater that night she'd lain awake feeling guilty about leading Benjamin to believe there was any chance of a relationship between them other than a working one. No matter how she looked at it, and as much as she enjoyed yesterday with him, there was no future in it.

She had so many things to do to prepare for her baby, starting with finding a place to live. As much as she appreciated Fred and Elsie's generosity, she would need a place of her own when the baby came. That would mean she'd have to find a fulltime job that she could rely upon. She loved the restaurant, but when the tourists left in a few weeks, she would probably be laid off.

On top of that, she had to find Kevan and tell him he was going to be a father. She'd promised herself that she would try to reach Julia, Kevan's sister, again today. If she had to, she'd disguise her voice to get past Mrs. McElroy.

She had thought about calling Cindy and asking her to help find Kevan, but she didn't want to do that. She couldn't let anyone back home in on the secret that she was pregnant. Yet, she could trust Cindy. Her contacts through her father could be helpful. He might be one of the few people outside the family who knew something of Kevan's whereabouts. And he'd do anything Cindy asked.

Walking quickly in the crisp morning air, she made it to the restaurant faster than she'd expected. Once inside, she spotted a man in painter's pants standing way back, away from the wall, his head cocked to one side. He turned as she approached.

"So…you're the lady who picked this color?" he asked.

"I am," she said, suddenly afraid to look, believing that the man's expression said it all.

"Well, I'm impressed," he said. "It took a little while to get the paintings level, but your diagram laid it all out for me. Have you been doing this sort of work for long?"

She stared at the wall, her heart thudding in her chest. The lights were perfectly positioned to show off the paintings. The size and placement of each work of art was just as she imagined it. "You did all this," she said in awe.

"I just followed your instructions."

Delighted with her efforts she viewed the wall from every angle. She had to admit that it was pretty nice for someone with little or no decorating experience except for her bedroom at home. *What would her mother and father think? Would they be pleased? Would they ever have a chance to see it?* The thought of being so far from home when something this good had happened made her feel sad and isolated.

"This is just what I wanted for the entrance. You've done a great job," Benjamin said, his voice so close it made her jump.

She turned around and found herself facing his chest. "You like it?"

"I think it's extraordinary. You took a very simple concept and made a wonderful wall display recognizing local artists. Thank you," he said.

"You're welcome." She had a sudden crazy urge to move into his arms, to be close to him and the feelings he created in her these last few days.

BENJAMIN FOUGHT the need to pull Sarah into his embrace. Hardly the behavior a boss should be exhibiting, but still and all, being around her had that effect on him. He'd spent last night tossing and turning, and trying to figure out what he should do where this woman was concerned.

Yet, as he looked into her eyes he knew exactly what he *wanted* to do. "You have real talent. I think we need to get a few business cards made up for you to use when people ask."

"I hadn't thought of having business cards made. Do you really think other people will want to hire me?" she asked, looking up into his face.

"You don't know how good you are at this sort of thing. Look what you did with the sandwich board. People often remark about how the board looks now, the way you've turned a meal offering into a story for all to read."

"It's so nice when people appreciate what I do."

"Have you always been interested in design?"

"Yes. As long as I can remember. My dad bought me a wooden table and chair set at a flea market. I sanded them down and repainted them. I turned each chair into a painted scene from different fairy tales. It was so much fun. I wanted to keep them, but my mother thought I should sell them."

"And did you?"

"Our neighbor two doors down."

"See? You'd already made your first sale before you got here."

She gave him a quirky grin, and he suddenly felt energized and happy.

"If I want this to be ready when we open I'd better get going. I'll organize the information about each artist along the table," she said, moving away from him.

He stood a few steps behind her, unwilling to leave her until he asked the question that had haunted him all night. "Sarah, earlier, when I asked how long you'd be staying here in Bar Harbor you said you'd be here at least until Christmas but weren't sure how long after that... I need to know."

He waited for her to say something, anything that would tell him what she was thinking.

"I want to live here...permanently. I love it here."

He felt as if a huge weight had been lifted off his shoulders. "As long as you want to live here you will always have a job in my restaurant. That's a promise."

Her hand went to her throat and she touched the gold chain; a look of amazement crossed her face. "You mean that?"

"I absolutely do."

Without saying a word, she moved closer to him and hugged him close; so close he could hardly breathe. But he really didn't care whether he breathed or not. As long as she held him like that he was happy.

"Sorry. I didn't mean to embarrass you," she said, stepping away.

"You could never embarrass me."

LATER, Sarah watched as people came past, their eyes taking in the wall of paintings. Their positive comments made her feel wonderful, and for the first time in months she felt really positive about her abilities.

In her new job as hostess, she greeted customers, and now many of them wanted to know about her, about her interest in design. She was flattered. She loved her new position, despite her earlier concern that she might be too shy to carry it off well.

She was watching Benjamin out of the corner of her eye when a woman with a little boy walked up to him and hugged him. He kissed her cheek, holding her in his arms as he clucked the little boy under the chin to squeals of delight. Then he took the little boy in his arms, hugged him close, and walked with the woman toward his office at the back of the restaurant.

Sarah watched, her stomach roiling, her heart drumming painfully in her chest. She knew he'd never been married, but no one mentioned that he had had a relationship and fathered a child. Or was she jumping to conclusions?

CHAPTER EIGHTEEN

She didn't see the woman or the child leave the restaurant, but Benjamin left early in the afternoon. Sarah finished her shift, leaving behind a totally booked-up evening for the staff to deal with. She let the person taking her place know what was going on, listened to her praise about the wall, then headed out onto the street alone.

She'd make one last call from the phone both to the McElroy residence on her way home. This call went the same as the other one, only this time she got as far as the maid, who offered no information when she asked about Kevan. Discouraged, she slumped against the wall of the phone booth. There was only one choice left to her. If she couldn't contact him, and he hadn't gotten in touch with her, she'd have to do what was best for her baby on her own.

Her head filled with thoughts about all the things she needed to do: her mind racing, she took a deep breath. With Benjamin's assurance that her job was safe, she would work on her family to convince to let her keep her baby. She could live at her aunt and uncle's until after the baby was born, and in the meantime, she'd find an apartment. Leslie Anne had offered to help.

She was just a couple of blocks from home when a truck pulled up to the curb beside her.

"Want a drive?" Benjamin asked, as he leaned over and opened the door.

"Thanks," she said, getting in.

He pulled ahead and drove into a parking lot, then shut off the engine without explanation. "What's going on?" she asked.

He gazed out the windshield, his arms resting on the wheel. "I... after yesterday I feel closer to you than I've felt to anyone in a long time. I know this sounds presumptuous, but I need your advice."

"Me?" she said, totally surprised. "Sure, if I can help you."

"I didn't get a chance to introduce you to my sister, Lilly. She came into the restaurant with her son today. She's going through a divorce and she wants to move back home so she can raise her son around family."

So that was the woman she saw earlier. "Is that a problem?"

He sighed and looked away. "It shouldn't be." He turned back to her. "I don't normally confide in people, and especially not people I don't know well. But I find myself wanting to talk to you."

She'd been feeling the same way about him these past couple of days. "How can I help?"

His gaze held hers, and for a few minutes it felt like they were in sync somehow.

"Ah... Here's the deal. I have always looked after my family. When my dad died, I moved Mom into a garden home where I thought she'd be happy. But she wasn't and she started making all sorts of demands on me, even cost me a relationship with a woman I was dating. When my sister got pregnant, I helped her out finan-cially." He rested his head on the steering wheel for a moment before continuing. "I feel like all I am is a person who helps others cope with their lives. And I'm really tired of it. I know that sounds like I'm really selfish, but if my sister does move home she will expect me to be there for her. I will. But when is it my turn?"

She understood what he was saying in a way he couldn't imagine. Not knowing how to explain her feelings, she touched his arm. "I'm sorry."

His eyes met hers, a sad smile forming on his lips. "What am I doing? Dumping all this on you. I have no right to burden you with my problems."

He needed her support. A sense of calm settled over her at the thought. She would help this man anyway she could. "No. You have every right. We're friends, and...I feel the same way. In the weeks since I moved here, I've come to realize how much I want to please my parents, even to the point of doing something I don't believe in. I don't know how to make them see that what they want will never work for me."

"Can I help?"

In those three words she knew that this man was much more to her than simply a friend. "I wish you could. I really do. But you've already done a whole lot for me by giving me a job, and encouraging me."

"I believe you'd do the same for me," he said.

She wanted to help him so much. "Does your sister plan to move in with your mom?"

"She'll expect me to find her a place to live, do all the work around her moving back. And then there's her son..." He tapped the steering wheel. "When I would rather be spending time with you, getting to know you, I will be dragged into my sister's problems. I don't want to do it, and I feel guilty for thinking that way."

"Does your sister have friends here who might be able to help her?"

"She's actually staying with a high school friend while she's here. It would certainly be nice if her friend could help."

"And much easier on you."

"It seems that trying to please family is something we share." His eyes searched her face, making her aware of how close she felt to him. "Sarah, I feel better just talking to you."

She'd never known a man who talked so openly about his feelings, and she knew what kind of courage that took. "I hope we can always talk this way."

"Yeah, especially now that you're living here." He sighed as he looked into her eyes. "But enough of all this. I had a great time with you yesterday. I was wondering if you'd like to go for a drive to Portland with me. I need to check out some restaurant appliances I'm thinking of buying."

"It would have to be on my day off."

"That could be arranged," he said, his warm smile lifting her spirits as it did so often these days.

"But I'm your employee, and I don't want the other staff feeling that I'm being given special treatment because we are doing things together."

"I understand. But is that how you see yourself where I'm concerned?"

What could she say? After hearing his worries about his sister, how could she ever confide in him about her problems? "We're becoming good friends. We've discovered things we share, things we like to do together."

"And that's enough...for now. Is that what you're saying?"

CHAPTER NINETEEN

a few days later Sarah had just settled into the easy routine of her work day when Benjamin approached her. "I'd like you to meet Lilly," he said, offering her that smile of his that always brightened her day.

Sarah felt a pang of anxiety at meeting his sister. What would the woman think of her? And why did it suddenly matter so much? "I'm pleased to meet you. I understand you've decided to move home."

"I have. Timothy, my son, and I have decided that this is where we belong." Lilly shifted her gaze to her brother. "And Benjamin has been a huge help."

Her gaze returning to Sarah, Lilly asked, "Would it be all right if you and I had a cup of coffee together? I'd like to get to know you a little better. Benjamin has talked so much about you."

"I would really like that, and it's my break time so I'm free for a bit," Sarah said, flattered that her boss had said nice things about her.

"Then, off we go to the coffee shop next door. Not trying to take business from my brother. Just want to talk without him peering at us," she teased.

When they got to the coffee shop they found a quiet table at the back and settled in.

"You have to know that I am really nosey about you," Lilly said. "My brother has been different since I got home, and the only thing that has changed in his life, that I can see, is you."

"How's he different?"

"He's happier. More upbeat. He is always talking about something you did, something you said."

"I really like your brother. He's so sweet and kind."

Lilly's eyes widened. "Is that so? That's wonderful. And I hear you've been out on *Moon Stone*. Not everyone is chosen to go out on his sailboat. You *are* special to him."

Lilly set back to allow the waiter to place the coffee and muffins in front of them. "Yes, my brother is super good to everyone he cares about. Look at me, for instance. I'm going through a nasty divorce. I'm finding it really hard, and quite frankly if I couldn't rely on Benjamin I don't know what I'd do."

"I can only imagine what you're going through," Sarah said, feeling a connection to this woman who was in the midst of something so painful...with a child involved.

"What about you? How did you end up in my brother's life? Mom and I have been trying to marry him off for years, and he's never once given us hope... Well except maybe with Miriam Dutcher, his girlfriend in high school and Mom's pick to become Mrs. Benjamin Patterson. But the way he talks about you, makes me wonder if maybe you're the reason he's changed."

"Your brother is a good friend to me. I enjoy working for him," she said, feeling a little awkward trying to explain a relationship she didn't really understand herself.

"Benjamin is a true-blue guy. He is caring, concerned and totally inarticulate when it comes to expressing his feelings."

"Really? I find talking to him so easy, and he tells me things about his life that I find interesting."

Lilly cocked one eyebrow. "Then you are making progress," she said in a wry tone. "Keep up the good work. I want my brother to find someone and soon, before he enters middle age."

"He's not that old," Sarah said, a little surprised.

"He's twenty-nine. That's old in the world of marriage, don't you think?"

"I suppose. But if he hasn't met the right person—"

"My point exactly. I'm hoping you're the right person."

Sarah didn't know what to say. She toyed with her coffee cup, remembering how often she and Benjamin had talked about things, shared things in the weeks she'd been working in his restaurant. She couldn't help but wonder how she would feel if ever things changed between them. "You're putting a lot of pressure on me," she said, trying to make a joke of it.

"I am. I want my brother to be happy. And he's been smiling a lot lately."

She liked this woman, and would be happy to have her as a friend. "Are you interested in interior decorating?"

Lilly looked surprised. "Yes. As a matter of fact, I am."

"Would you like to go to the fabric store on Sutter Street with me some time?"

"Are you looking for something special?"

"No. I just love to look, get ideas, things like that."

"I'd like to do that too. Mom's house needs a little updating, and at one time I was pretty good with a sewing machine. Looking at fabrics is a great idea."

Later the next day they met up and went to the fabric place, spending an enjoyable couple of hours in which Sarah learned about Benjamin's life as a teenager, his love of rock music and his interest in space exploration. Spending time with Lilly had been among the best times she'd had since she moved there.

She was happy to be making new friends.

THE NEXT WEEK Benjamin offered her a drive home every day, something that was becoming a pattern. They talked about work, the interesting patrons at the restaurant, but mostly about his sister.

"Life is full of change, isn't it?" he asked.

"We can't know the future, or what we'll be doing six weeks from now. We can only deal with now."

"How did you get to be so wise, Miss Maddison?" he asked, his tone light and teasing.

"Hanging around you did it to me," she said.

"I'm so pleased I'm having an effect on you."

As they pulled into the driveway he turned to her. "Thank you for listening."

"You're welcome," she said, so aware of him, of sitting near him in the cab of his truck in a quiet space – the kind of space she would need if things went the way she feared when she told her family she was determined to keep her baby.

"I'll see you at work tomorrow," he said.

As she met his gaze, she realized that she wanted to talk to him, to share things with him. She was so grateful to have him in her life. "I look forward to it," she said.

"Have a good evening," he said, leaning across her to open her door.

She watched him drive away. There was nothing more she could do where Kevan was concerned. What she did next had to be for her baby's sake.

She entered the house to the sound of clapping. "Leah Trimble, down at the post office, says that you did a beautiful job displaying her work. You're getting a name for yourself," Fred said, smiling as he brought a dish to the table. "We are having a celebration dinner tonight to honor your artistic talents."

She listened to them talk in glowing terms about her job, her design work and how well she was doing – to the point where she wondered if there was something they hadn't told her.

"Sarah, honey, you know how much we love you. How much we want you to be happy. We've had several talks around what you will do when your baby comes, but not about you." He glanced over at Elsie before continuing. "We wondered if you planned to stay here after the adoption, or whether you planned to go back home. Why we're asking is that we're giving thought to renovating the summer kitchen at the back of the house, that has mostly been used for storage. It was part of the house in colonial days, but hasn't been really useful for us where it's just the two of us."

"What are you saying?"

"We wondered if you might be interested in the suite of rooms we're planning to make out of the space. You don't have to tell us just yet. Think about it. We know you have a lot on your mind."

"I thought you were going to move to something smaller, not make this bigger."

Elsie touched her shoulder, patting it awkwardly. "We've been talking, and we are worried about you, about how you will cope when you give up your baby. We wondered if you planned to move back home and go to Hastings next year?"

"I have been waiting for a chance to talk to you both, to see if I can get your support where Mom and Dad are concerned. You see, I can't give up my baby. I know that's not what you want to hear, and it's definitely not what Mom and Dad want to hear." She glanced from one to the other. "But I have a job, one that will be permanent. I've started to do a little interior decorating work. I have a good friend who is willing to help me. I'm happy with my life. And my life includes my baby."

Elsie stepped back, pressing her fingers to her mouth as she glanced at Fred. Fred fiddled with the chain on his pocket watch. The clock clunked once before chiming. Patches stared up at Sarah before winding his body around her legs.

"Have you told your parents any of this?" Elsie asked.

"They're trying to do what they believe is best for me, but I can't let my baby go." She saw the pain in their eyes, and remembered her mother telling her about the three babies her aunt and uncle had lost early in their marriage.

She wanted them to understand so badly. "What would you do if you were me? I realize that I don't have a husband to support me, but I am more than willing to work hard, to make a life for my baby and me. If you were me, could you give up your baby?"

Elsie relented first. "No, we couldn't. But we worry about hard this will be for you."

CHAPTER TWENTY

After talking to her aunt and uncle, Sarah couldn't sleep. She got up early, cleaned up her room and fed Patches. Even patting her cat, and listening to his soothing purr didn't ease the anxiety that enveloped her. She had taken a stand for her baby. She had told her aunt and uncle her plan to raise her baby on her own. And now she had to make it all happen. Her worry now was whether or not she could do it.

As the sun slashed a bright yellow strip along the horizon she found herself walking along the waterfront, out toward the marina to the place where she'd had her first glimpse of what life on a sailboat was like. A pleasant memory offering her a moment's reprieve.

She walked along the sandy beach on the other side of the marina, formulating a plan as she listened to the soft rustling of the waves foaming along the beach. She was standing there facing the rising sun when she heard someone calling her name. She turned and saw Benjamin coming toward her.

"What are you doing down here so early?" he asked, as he approached, the sun glinting off his freshly showered dark hair.

"I couldn't sleep. I decided to go for a walk before I went to work."

"We're both up early worrying, is that it? But if the call I got last evening is any indication, you're about to feel a whole lot better about things."

"Call?"

"Yes. I had a call from a business associate, Mark Saunders. He owns Harborside Inn, up the coast a few miles. He wants to revamp the dining room once the tourist season is over for the year. He heard about what you did for me, and wondered if you would be willing to meet with him. What do you think?"

She went to him, her heart singing in delight. "I would love it," she said, teetering on the rocky outcropping in the sand. "Should I call him?"

He nodded. "Mark is expecting you to call today."

"I've never done this before. What will I tell him? How do I know what I should charge him?" she asked, looking up into Benjamin's face.

"Let's walk for a few minutes while I tell you my plan." He took her hand in his, his skin warm on hers.

Happiness welled up in her. "What should I do?" she asked, aware of how much she wanted his advice and support as she considered this new opportunity.

"After your shift today, we'll sit down and figure out a few prices for the various steps in what you'd do for Mark. I don't know much about design work. But I do know that you've got tons of potential and a chance here to start your own business."

She hugged his arm in happiness. "Thank you, Benjamin, so much. I couldn't do this without you, and I want to be successful doing this."

His steps slowed as his arm slipped around her shoulders, "I would do anything for you, Sarah. I love spending time with you. I think I've made that clear. I know this probably doesn't sound right, that I'm trying to get a commitment from you to see me as more than a friend by offering to help you. But I want you to know that I will help you regardless of whether our relationship moves further."

She held her breath. "What are you saying?"

"I like you. A lot. I want more than a friendship with you," he said, his tone certain.

Her eyes met his, and in that moment, she saw a man she had come to care about and respect. A man who made her feel happy every time she saw him. A man who seemed a lot like Kevan...

"I want one with you as well," she said and watched his expression brighten in response.

"This is great news," he said quickly, pulling her into his arms, and kissing the breath from her lips.

He held her gently, his scent melding with the sudden rush of desire flowing through her. She reached up and pulled him closer. Drowning in her desire for him she ignored the little voice in her head. The one that kept saying, Kevan.

As he kissed her Benjamin felt something...as if it were a missing part, like a jigsaw puzzle piece, dropped into place in his life. He held her closer, feeling the soft curve of her body beneath her jacket. He held her head in his hands, looking straight into her eyes.

"Who knows how this will work out between us. You already know my track record where women are concerned. But right now, all that matters is how happy you've made me."

"Me too," she whispered, her fingers stroking his cheek, driving his need for her, for more moments of closeness with this woman who had become so important to him.

"Sarah, I feel so different with you in my life. I can't explain it, only that I feel at ease around you. That no matter what is going on in my life, whenever you smile at me I feel better." He suddenly felt embarrassed. "Right now, I'm saying things to you I've never said to

111

another woman. Couldn't show how I felt. But with you, it seems so natural."

Her eyes searched his face, her smile gentle on her lips. "I feel the same way. We are so comfortable with each other. Life seems so easy when we're together," she said.

He pulled her close to him, feeling her warmth, the scent of her... Something floral and very pleasant. He felt her shiver. "Are you cold? Or simply excited by what we're doing? I feel excited. We have so much ahead of us. So many ways to learn about each other." He smiled down at her. "This is what I want. You are what I want," he said, his words flowing from him, yet using words that were not normally his...would never have been said by him to any other woman.

"I'm excited too, but shouldn't we be getting to the restaurant?" She took his hand, turned his wrist and looked at his watch. "I should have been there ten minutes ago."

He chuckled. "We're taking a giant step in our relationship. A few minutes won't matter. Besides, the boss will understand." He winked playfully, feeling better than he'd felt in years. "But yes; we'd better get a move on. My truck is over there." He pointed to the parking lot adjacent to the marina.

THEY WORKED all day in the restaurant. Yet, Sarah was having trouble keeping her mind on her job as she played back every moment she'd shared with Benjamin that morning. Leslie Anne came up beside her at the desk. "What is going on with you? You're on another planet today."

"Do you think other people have noticed?" she asked, glancing around.

"They'd have to be blind not to," Leslie Anne said. "Tell me what's going on with you."

"I've just had so much happen in the past few hours." She told

Leslie Anne about her conversation with her aunt and uncle last evening, her news from Benjamin about the inn wanting her design help.

"Okay. I agree. You've had a lot happening, but there's more isn't there?"

"Benjamin and I are dating."

"That's not news," Leslie Anne said.

"I mean officially dating."

Leslie Anne's eyes widened. "As in with some form of commitment?"

She nodded, feeling again the warmth of his arms, the urgency of his kiss.

"Have you told him about your situation?"

Sarah glanced around to see if anyone was listening. "Keep your voice down."

"Well, have you?" she whispered.

"No. There doesn't seem to be a good moment."

"With that kind of news there never will be. Are you going to keep seeing him and not tell him? You're going to be showing pretty soon."

With her friend's words her happy world slowly dissolved around her. She hadn't thought any further than the happiness she'd experienced when Benjamin and she had decided to date. She had let herself believe that somehow her circumstances were not real, that the baby was not part of the relationship. But her and Kevan's baby would be part of her life forever.

What was she thinking? She has feelings for another man. And she was having another man's child. A man she said she'd love forever... Had promised to wait for...

"What am I going to do?" she asked her friend.

"When is your next appointment with your doctor?"

"Oh my gosh! It's this afternoon after my shift, and I promised

Benjamin that I would work with him to come up with a proposal for the project at the inn. What am I going to do?"

"If it were me, I'd see my doctor, talk to her about everything, and maybe that will help you decide what to do."

Crestfallen, Sarah glanced toward the back of the restaurant. Benjamin was standing there, his eyes on her, a gentle smile on his face. Taking a deep breath, she started toward him, disappointment dogging her every step. She would tell him she couldn't meet with him after work, that something had come up. It was a small lie, but one that was necessary to keep her secret, for a little longer.

CHAPTER TWENTY-ONE

$\mathcal{H}$er appointment with the doctor went well. According to Dr. Harding, she and her baby were doing well. The doctor encouraged her to eat healthy and to continue getting exercise. She offered no advice in whether she should keep her baby.

As she walked home, there was only one person she hadn't asked to help her: Cindy. She'd be in university, her first term, now, and Sarah missed her. She and Cindy had never been apart this long before. What she wouldn't give to talk to Cindy the way they used to do. She felt so much guilt about hiding the truth from her. She was hiding the truth from so many people who mattered to her, including Benjamin.

She didn't like hiding the truth from Benjamin either. But she didn't know what to do or how to tell him the truth. Leslie Anne was right. How could she have a relationship with a man who had been honest with her while she'd kept the most important information about her from him?

As she entered the house, she heard a loud thump. Patches landed on the floor and came toward her, emitting a loud purr.

"Come here, big guy," she said, scooping him up and rubbing the narrow space between his ears.

Walking toward the kitchen she smelled the scent of freshly baked molasses cookies. Her aunt slid a cookie sheet out of the oven and onto the cooling rack. "Glad you're home, dear," she said, putting the oven mitts on the counter before coming around the island toward her. "I'm sorry about our earlier talk. We do understand what a difficult decision you have to make."

Fred came down the back stairs into the kitchen. "And we've decided that we will fix up the space we talked about and it is yours if you want it."

"You mean it?" Sarah asked, tears starting behind her eyelids at the thought that her plans had a chance of working out. "I...I don't know what to say." She went to them, hugging them both as she sobbed into their arms. "I've been so worried about what I am going to do when I have my baby. Now at least, I can think about the future without wondering where we will live." She stepped back, smiled at them, and said, "I will pay rent, you understand?"

"We'll work something out," Uncle Fred said.

"No. I'm serious. I may not be able to pay what someone else might pay, but I want to pay you. I won't be a charity case," she said, her body weak with relief.

"Whatever you say," Aunt Elsie murmured as she reached up and stroked Sarah's cheek. "You are like the daughter we never had. We want what you want."

"Thank you so much. You will not be sorry."

"How did your doctor's appointment go?" Elsie asked.

"It was fine. She's a really nice doctor," Sarah said.

With a new sense of purpose, she cleaned up the kitchen after dinner and went to her room. When she got to the top of the stairs she went to the wall phone and called Cindy's home number. Her mother Blanche answered on the first ring. "Mrs. Underhill, it's Sarah, I'm looking for Cindy's number at college."

"Hi Sarah. It's so good to hear from you," Blanche said, tentatively. "How are you doing in your nursing program? Is it busy?"

"It's going well," she lied, her stomach burning. "I need to talk to Cindy."

"I'll give you her number. She'd love to hear from you," Blanche said, before reading off the number.

Before she could make her call to Cindy the phone rang. She picked it up. "Sarah, it's Benjamin. I was hoping to help you with your proposal for Mark Saunders this afternoon, but I understand you had an appointment you had to keep. I was wondering if you'd be willing to work the evening shift tomorrow? We are a little short-handed due to three people coming down with the flu. Unless I find another waiter, you might have to serve tables as well."

She listened to his voice, his calmness easing her anguish. It seemed that every time she was feeling upset or uncertain, Benjamin was there. "Sure. I can come in for the evening shift"

"Are you okay? You sound like you have a cold. You're not getting the flu, are you?"

"No. I'm fine," she said, "but thank you for being concerned."

"I am always concerned about you," he said.

"I hope that someday I can do something nice for you."

"Coming in tomorrow evening is something nice you'll be doing for me."

"I mean something special, only for you," she said.

There was only silence from Benjamin. Had she said something wrong? Was he uncomfortable with what she'd said?

"Sarah, no one makes that kind of offer to me. It's usually the other way around. Thank you. You being part of my life is special to me. You know that."

She breathed a sigh of relief. "I do. And I am here if you need me."

"That's really great. After work tomorrow evening we'll talk about a few ideas I have for your proposal to Mark about his inn."

After she hung up, it came to her. She wanted him to need her in a personal way, the way she needed him. Maybe if they both needed each other, she could tell him the truth about everything. And how she longed to do that and to have him then choose to remain a part of her life.

CHAPTER TWENTY-TWO

The next day, feeling both unsettled and excited by Benjamin's words she hadn't followed through on calling Cindy. There simply hadn't been a moment when she could sit down and concentrate on talking to her friend. She could rely on Cindy to keep her secret, of that much she was certain. But she was not sure how Cindy would respond to a call from her after all this time.

Yet, she needed to make the call for so many reasons, and she would do it tonight, after she got home. She gathered her things and headed for the restaurant, weaving her way around the throngs of tourists filling the streets. When she reached the restaurant's back entrance, she opened the door and ran smack into Benjamin.

"I'm here, and on time," she said, trying for a teasing tone.

"How're you doing?" he asked, his eyes focused solely on her.

"I'm good. Spent the morning doing housework things, and working on my proposal to Mark in between giving Patches, my cat, lots of attention. What about you?"

"Busy. Busy. I didn't know you had a cat. I have one too. Tinker Bell." He smiled at her, a smile that felt warm and inclusive. "Lilly named him. He was her cat until she moved to New York. Lucky for me she can have him back now."

"One of the good things about her moving home?"

"Yeah. That and Mom being happy to have family around. Where did you get your cat?"

"Patches was a homeless kitten living on the streets."

He looked at her for a minute. "And you rescued him." His gentle laughter eased along her spine, setting up a tingling sensation. Moments of closeness and gentle humor, she hadn't imagined possible when she first met him. But most of all, there was connection she could no longer deny.

"Yes, I rescued him. And I love him. I brought him with me."

"Part of your entourage?" he kidded.

"Absolutely." She wanted to stay there and enjoy his company, but being this close to him also made her feel confused, conflicted.

"I'd better go," she said, suddenly not wanting him to see how vulnerable she felt around him…how exposed. When she'd put on her uniform today it was tight across her tummy. Her baby was growing. She had to tell Benjamin about it, and soon.

She had lied to all her friends at home and given up her chance to go to college. She didn't intend to ruin this relationship with a lie. She needed Ben's approval and caring, or to end her personal relationship with him now.

She would try to tell him tonight; would trust that he would have a job for her once she was showing. But underneath all that was the fear that when she told him about her baby he would not be interested in her. That he might think she actually didn't tell him in order to keep her job. That wasn't true. It wasn't just about the job. She wanted him in her life along with his approval and caring. Yet, a part of her feared that she would lose both when she told him her secret.

He looked quizzically at her. "Are you all right?"

"Yes, of course." Her stomach churned at the thought of what she had to do.

"I'm relieved to hear that." He leaned closer. "If everything is good with you why don't you meet me tonight in my office when you're finished? We won't be long putting your proposal for Mark Saunders together."

"I would like that very much," she said.

BENJAMIN WATCHED her walk away from him through the corridor linking the service area with the restaurant. He was pleased they'd bumped into each other. Every time he saw her he felt excited – happy even, and that was a heady feeling for him, a man who'd thought life would just be work, work, work.

The rest of the evening passed in a blur of greeting people, checking the flow of food to the tables, ensuring that all went smoothly, his usual night at the restaurant. Yet, he was impatient for it to be over. When Sarah finished her shift, he was waiting near the bar as they began to close up, trying to look busy and failing completely. For the past hour he'd watched for her, smiling when their eyes met, nodding when she glanced his way.

"How did your evening go?" he asked, knowing full well that she had worked very hard.

She swiped a strand of hair off her cheek, letting out a long sigh. "I am exhausted. What about you?"

"Not as bad as you, obviously. Let's get a soda from the cooler and go up to my office so we can talk. By the way, two other people made a point of telling me this evening how much they liked your wall collage."

"That's great," she said, walking beside him, her body brushing against his several times.

As they reached the office, he opened the door, and signaled her to go in ahead of him. She took the chair across the desk from him, the exhaustion in her eyes tearing at him.

"You're really tired. We can wait and do this tomorrow when you've had a little rest. We could go out for lunch tomorrow since you'll be working tomorrow evening again."

"That would be nice," she said, yet her eyes didn't meet his.

He didn't mean to stare at her, but she didn't seem to be feeling very well. "You're sure you're all right?" he asked.

"Yes. It's just been a really long day and maybe I should go home."

"Let me drive you," he said, wanting to be with her a little longer, if only to be sure she was okay.

"Thank you."

He got her out to the truck, unlocked the door and helped her in. As she leaned back in the seat she gave a little gasp. "Oh!"

"Sarah, you're not well," he said, instantly worried that she might need to go to the hospital.

"No. I'm fine. Really. It feels like I twisted something."

When he got in the truck she was rubbing her stomach and sitting at an awkward angle in the seat.

"Do you have pain? Do you need something to eat?"

She glanced over at him, her eyes dark pools in the low light of the truck cab. "I...I have something to tell you, and you're probably not going to like it."

Was she quitting? Did she not want to go out with him again? Please, no.

He had been so happy the last couple of weeks, weeks in which his thoughts so often went to the woman sitting beside him.

"You can tell me anything, Sarah. I'm here for you, no matter what."

CHAPTER TWENTY-THREE

*H*ow was she going to say the words she had to say? She'd dreaded this moment, but now that it was here, she felt panic rising up through her. How would she tell this man who'd been so kind to her about her secret? A man who would almost certainly be upset with her. After all, he'd taken her on, and liked her work, but how would he feel now – if she had to quit to have a baby…

"There is no easy way to say this. I am expecting a baby," she said, not looking at him for fear she'd see condemnation in his eyes.

"You're…having a baby? Is there someone in your life, the father of your baby?"

"No. No." She wiped her hands across her face, trying to figure out how to say what she needed to say. "I didn't tell you about my past because at first I thought you wouldn't hire me. Then I thought you'd be angry at me for deceiving you."

She looked at him, at the anxiety in his eyes, and wished with all her heart she didn't need to continue. "Worst of all, my family are upset with me. They expect me to give up my baby. I can't do that, but they are insisting."

Taking a deep breath to steady her nerves she continued. "The father of my baby has gone to Ireland. I haven't heard from him since he left." A cold shiver ran through her at the loss she'd experienced, that she continued to experience.

"Did you call the police?"

"His family know where he is. They won't tell me. If I try to press them for information I believe they will call in my father's loan on their house, maybe even fire my parents. I can't let that happen. And now... Oh. Oh. This is so awful. You must think I'm an idiot."

"No. Not at all. You're in a tough situation."

"Are you angry at me?"

"*What?* No. I'm just surprised that you didn't tell me sooner," he said.

"You mean that?"

He nodded.

She reached across the console that separated them. "No one has been as kind to me as you have. Thank you."

He took her hand in his, a strong hand that offered so much reassurance. "Sarah, I'm sorry this happened to you. I wish I'd known sooner, but I understand how difficult all this is for you. You've been abandoned to face this situation, and the man involved should be found and made to make restitution."

"What do you suggest I do?" she asked.

"What do *we* do, you mean?"

At his words her heart rose in her throat. In the middle of the worst time of her life this man was there for her. "Are you sure you want to be involved in this, in my life?" Her voice shook as relief flooded her.

"From the beginning," he whispered and tipping her face up he kissed her.

She was lost in the moment of sheer joy, of knowing that Benjamin was there for her, for what she would face in the months to come. He rubbed her back, his fingers easing the tension that had been with her for so long. "That feels so good," she murmured against his throat.

"It's my specialty," he said, kissing her forehead as he continued to rub her shoulders.

"You're hired," she whispered tilting her face up, her lips searching for his.

They kissed gently yet firmly. Her head spun with happiness and relief.

After a few minutes, he pulled away from her. "I would love to continue what we're doing, but first I want to talk about your future."

"I can't continue as a waitress once I really start to show, can I?"

"No. My customers are old fashioned that way, and this is Maine, not New York," he said, ruefully. "But we have to find a way to make it easier for you to work until your baby comes."

"What would that be? I couldn't work in the office. I don't have any office skills."

He tapped the steering wheel, his eyes never leaving her face. "Most evenings I manage the restaurant, but with the latest apartment building I've purchased, my workload has increased. What if I offer you the job of evening supervisor."

"What would I do? What would be involved?"

"You'd do what I've been doing. You'd keep an eye on customer flow, any line ups at the door. You'd be the person staff would come to if they ran out of something or had an issue that had to be dealt with during the shift. You've been doing some of it as the evening hostess. I'd show you the rest of it. You could do it."

She looked at him. "Are you sure...? You'd do this just for me?"

"You mean a great deal to me. And to think that someone could abandon you this way." He shook his head, his eyes sad. "I wish I'd known, but now that I do, we'll work this out."

A sob rose in her throat as the pent-up stress eased from her shoulders. "Thank you," she murmured, wanting to climb into his arms and stay there.

"You're welcome."

They talked for hours about her hopes and dreams for her baby. He told her how much he wanted children. That he would do whatever he could to help. He stopped short of admitting how deep his feelings went for her. Not because he didn't want to, but because he didn't know how she would react. He would do what he could to help her and see if she returned his feelings.

For Sarah, it felt like she had come home, safe with a man who cared, who would help her have her child while providing her with a job. She couldn't ask for more. And for now, she didn't want more.

CHAPTER TWENTY-FOUR

The next morning, she woke up knowing that more than anything she wanted to tell Cindy about her life, her future plans and apologize to her for not telling her the truth. She didn't know how Cindy would react when she told her everything, but she'd reached the point where she had to trust that her friend would understand. And if Cindy could forgive her for not telling her the truth, they would have a chance to be friends again. And if Cindy could help her, she might be able to find a way to reach Kevan.

Being part of Benjamin's life, she now realized that she had to settle her past if she could. She and Benjamin deserved to look toward the future, and that future included her baby. She also owed it to Kevan to try one last time to find him and tell him what had happened. After that it would be up to him to decide if he wanted to be part of the baby's life.

It was Saturday, a day Cindy's mom said she didn't have classes, and Sarah hoped she'd be around her dorm room and free to talk. Whether or not Cindy would forgive her for how she'd behaved could determine whether or not they might renew their friendship.

Thankfully her aunt and uncle were away for the day, leaving her with the house to herself. They'd started the renovation of the summer kitchen, and were off to Portland to look at finishing materials. The apartment would have two bedrooms, one of which she would make into a nursery by choosing a soft color for the walls and finding a bassinet and a chest of drawers for her baby.

She dialed the number and when a woman answered, Sarah knew instantly that it was Cindy. Her stomach quaked with apprehension. "Cindy, it's me. I'm sorry. So sorry. I want to apologize to you. I haven't been in touch, but my life has been a little hectic here."

"Sarah," Cindy breathed. "Where are you?"

Afraid of what would happen next, Sarah said, "I'm in Bar Harbor."

"What?"

"I'm in Bar Harbor. I am at my aunt and uncle's place, and I'm working in a restaurant downtown. I've been here since I graduated. I... Kevan and I are having a baby."

"Are you serious? Why didn't you tell me this before?" Cindy asked. "You left me and went off without a word of explanation, and now you tell me you're pregnant. How could you do this to us? I thought we were best friends. Was it because of what I told you?"

"No. I couldn't tell you the truth. My parents didn't want anyone to know that I was expecting a baby. Then I couldn't reach Kevan, and I still can't. It's been horrible." She forced herself to go on. "I have been trying to find the courage to talk to you, to see if you could forgive me..."

Tears clouded her vision as she continued: "I've been trying to make a life here. I've been to the doctor and my baby is healthy and growing. I felt the baby kick yesterday. That made it all so real. And yet I couldn't share it with you. And I feel terrible about that. This morning I decided to call you, to tell you the truth."

"Does anyone in the McElroy family know about this?"

"No! Kevan doesn't either."

"Why not?" Cindy said.

"Because I can't find him. I've tried. I heard from Mom that Kevan is working for his father in Ireland."

She went on to explain the threat Tom McElroy had made toward her parents, and what that meant to her chances of getting in touch with Kevan.

Cindy sighed. "I can't believe this is happening to you. Why didn't you tell me? I would have kept your secret."

"I promised Mom and Dad. They have done everything they could to help me, and I couldn't go against their wish that I tell no one. Not telling you was one of the hardest things I've ever done," Sarah confessed. "I miss you so much. I do. My life is lonely without you in it."

"Me too. I'm having a really hard time at college and I haven't made any friends. I've been going home on weekends but none of my friends are there anymore. They've all gone off to college or have new jobs and friends of their own."

"Do you think you might be able to visit me?" Sarah asked.

"I would love to. But school is much harder than I expected so I have to study a lot. We could get together at Thanksgiving. You'll be coming home, won't you?"

"I can't. I'll be showing by then…"

"And your mom and dad don't want anyone to know. I hear you. What can we do?"

"Do you suppose you could come here on your Thanksgiving break? Or a few days before Thanksgiving?"

"I've already promised Mom and Dad that I'll be home for Thanksgiving dinner." Cindy sighed in resignation. "But I'd rather spend time with you, see how you're doing. How are you going to reach Kevan? He needs to know he's going to be a father."

"Do you think your dad could find out anything about where he lives, or get his address or his phone number? Although Mom works in the administration office, she can't access his phone number in Ireland. Mom says he should be back here doing the right thing where I'm concerned and I believe if he knew, he would be."

"Let me see what I can find out. Given how controlling Mr. McElroy is, I doubt he's left Kevan's phone number lying around, but I'll talk to Dad and see."

"That would be great. Kevan needs to know about the baby."

"Sarah, what if his life has changed? It's been months. You haven't heard from him."

Until Cindy said the words, Sarah had been too fearful to think what it would mean if Kevan didn't come back to her and the baby once he found out. She'd been holding out for him, wanting him to be with her. She hadn't, until that moment, faced the possibility that Kevan wouldn't want to come home, and if he did, would he even want their child?

"I have to believe that when Kevan learns about me and our baby he will be on the next plane back here. Promise me you'll do everything you can to find Kevan's number."

"I will. And I'll come to visit you in Bar Harbor and not tell anyone. Well, except my parents. I can hardly run off during the Thanksgiving holiday without saying where I'm going."

"That's wonderful. Thank you so much. Will you call me at my Uncle Fred's when you find out something?"

"Sure."

Sarah read off the phone number.

"Sarah, I'll call you when I have something. I miss you."

Sarah felt the ache start in her chest and move up to her throat, an ache that had been there since that day on the steps of Harrison's Pharmacy. "I miss you too. See you Thanksgiving."

CHAPTER TWENTY-FIVE

The next week Sarah became the evening manager of the restaurant. After a few disconcerted looks from other staff members she settled into a routine of coming to work in the evening after a day filled with growing excitement. During the weeks that followed she finished the decorating plan to redo the interior of the restaurant, something she felt needed to be done to compliment the wall she'd created. She stayed late to help the crew of painters and floor finishers, do their jobs. Due to her careful planning the restaurant stayed open every day but one during the renovation period, something Benjamin praised her for.

With his help word got out and she'd been offered several other interior decorating jobs. She started with the Harborside Inn project, followed by another that drew on her skills to redesign a space. She was a little overwhelmed by all of it, but Benjamin was there to support her, offer her advice and tease her a little about being Superwoman.

Her parents had come to visit each month, surprised at how well she was doing. They had yet to agree that they were okay with her decision to keep her baby. Although her aunt and uncle still didn't talk about her decision they completed the apartment. She painted the second bedroom a soft shade of yellow and had gone looking for a bassinet and chest of drawers with Leslie Anne.

Despite everything it was as if no one in her family wanted to discuss the subject of her baby's future. Sarah hadn't brought it up again because she didn't want to face another argument with her parents.

She had waited near the phone for days after her call with Cindy, hoping that her friend would call with Kevan's number, but gradually as the weeks moved past, she'd stopped hovering and returned once again to her routine. A very pleasant routine in which she'd grown into her new job, had gained the respect of the restaurant staff and the suppliers she dealt with. She was getting to be a very capable business woman and she loved it.

With Thanksgiving only days away, and so many things going on, she hadn't had time to worry about the future. Besides, her future was looking pretty good, thanks in large part to Benjamin.

They were about to close up for the night when Benjamin came out of his office, and went to the bar where she was tallying up the night's receipts. They'd gotten into the habit of having a late supper together before the cook went off duty. The evening had been so busy that the cook had put the food on plates, ready for the microwave, before he left for the night.

This time was reserved for the two of them to catch up on work, and the projects each of them was involved in. Gradually it had become much more. They often talked for hours over their meal, hours that gradually became more about them than their work. Tonight would be no different, and she looked forward to the certainty of it.

"I'll get the plates ready and bring them to our table," he said, touching her shoulder in passing before heading to the kitchen.

She was waiting in their usual booth when he returned. She looked up into his handsome face as he brought a tray of food, utensils and sodas to the table, noting how comfortable she'd become with his caring and concern for her. "I'm starved," she said.

"How's Ben junior doing?" They'd slipped into the habit of talking about her baby as if it were a boy.

"Ben is just fine. In fact, he's been very active tonight, and my back is killing me," she said, rubbing her lower back.

"Want me to rub your back for you?" he asked.

She glanced over at him and saw the serious expression on his face. "It's okay. Sitting down will help. But I will be glad to climb into bed tonight." As she said the words out loud to this man who had come to mean so much to her, she was aware of the intimacy shared in the way they behaved with each other.

As she watched him she realized that he was acting more like a husband, than a dear friend...and it felt nice, if a little unsettling. Did he mean to behave that way? Or were they just friends that would do anything for each other?

"Have you heard back from your friend with Kevan's phone number?" he asked.

"No. Nothing." She sighed as she tackled her food with gusto.

"You *are* hungry. I can see that," he said, passing her the pepper.

"Thanks. By the way, I've been coming in a few minutes early each day, and discovered something that might mean more business for us."

"What's that?"

She put her fork down, leaning toward him in her eagerness to explain her idea. "With the new technical school here in town, there are a lot of students looking for take-out meals."

"Aren't they happy with pizzas and burgers?" he asked, his eyes on her in that unnerving way of his. The intensity unsettled her in the beginning. But she'd come to realize that it was part of Benjamin, a part she now found reassuring.

"I've asked the staff to keep count of the number of young people coming into the restaurant wanting to get take-out, and I believe it's enough for us to consider opening a take-out window where they can order their food. It will mean we'll also need a number they could call."

He rested his hands on the table. "Sarah, do you know how many times you said 'we'?"

She frowned. "What's that got to do with what I'm telling you? I use 'we' a lot. Always have."

"Just a comment. But to do what you're suggesting... It might be possible to work something out."

"And some of the tourists in the summer would take advantage of it as well. With a take-out window we'd get added business from those not willing to wait in line for a table, or who didn't want to eat inside. What to do you think?" she pressed.

"I think I'd like to not talk business tonight." He picked up his fork and began to eat.

"Okay. I understand." She didn't understand at all. Benjamin *always* wanted to talk business. He'd been out this afternoon when she got to work, claiming he had an appointment somewhere in town. He hadn't said where or for what. Was he seeing a doctor? Was he ill?

Her tummy did an anxious flip. He couldn't be sick. He couldn't. Yet, he had so much to look after, things she knew nothing about.

They ate for a few minutes before Benjamin suddenly put his fork down and leaned over the table toward her. "Sarah, I can't do this any longer."

Her heart shrunk in her chest. Her pulse jumped. "I don't understand. Are you ill?"

"Me? No! I'm fine."

"Do you want me to leave? I thought we were working so well together."

"No. Everything is fine. Just fine. It's me. I can't go on like *this*."

She looked at him, trying to figure out what he was talking about.

He made circles on the table with his fingers for a few minutes, then focused his attention on her. "Sarah, we have a good thing going here. Look at how well we get along in the restaurant, all the time we spend together. We both love what we do. Your career as an interior decorator is expanding. I've helped you. You've helped me so much. We are as close as two people can be without being married. I want a more permanent relationship with you. I want much more than simply being really good friends."

She looked at him…at the way his dark hair framed his face, the high forehead, the spidery lines of exhaustion visible around his eyes, the rich fullness of his lips. She knew in that instant that this man meant much more to her than she'd ever admitted to anyone. Every time she needed something: advice, a shoulder to lean on, and the fact that he always checked in with her, even on her days off. He'd even bought a car for her use, on the excuse that she needed reliable transportation. And she was delighted with the independence the car offered her.

Despite whatever Benjamin might be hinting at, sometime in the next few months she would give birth to her and Kevan's child, and then everything would change. Her first priority would be her baby. "You're right. We are as close as two people can be, and I never want to lose that closeness. We are a team in so many ways."

"Yes. Because of you my businesses are thriving. And that's because I can rely on you to manage things here. Look at the number of times you've come to work during your off hours. How many times have I been able to leave here, go to another of my businesses, secure in the idea that you have everything under control?"

"Are we talking about a business partnership?" She'd never considered that, although it would be wonderful to have that kind of financial security for her baby.

He placed his arms on the table on either side of his plate and said, "You goose. I'm asking you to marry me."

135

"Marriage? Benjamin, there is so much of my life that is not settled. In a few months I'm going to have a baby, and I have yet to find Kevan and tell him. We can't possibly talk about marriage until I've gotten my life sorted out," she said, surprised by his offer, and even more surprised that she didn't say no.

Benjamin took her hand in his. "Sarah, if you loved Kevan, you and I wouldn't be this close to each other. Over the months we've formed a bond that both of us want and need. I understand your concern to find Kevan, but he's not the one here caring for you, looking out for you *and* your baby. I'm here. I love you. Please stop looking for obstacles. It's really this simple. Do you love me enough to marry me?"

Words of love were on her lips, but was it love or gratitude?

"And would you be the father of my child? Would you risk that even when we don't know if Kevan is coming back to claim his baby? And then there are my parents who still haven't accepted my decision about my baby. I have to settle things with them about what I'm doing."

"And it would be so much easier for you, for both of us, if they knew you were going to be part of my life, that we were going to be a couple raising the baby together, wouldn't it?"

"You want me to accept your proposal as a way to get my parents to accept my decision about my baby?"

"No! Of course not. You need to resolve your issues with your family in whatever way works for you."

She saw the expectation in his eyes, and wanted to tell him what he needed to hear. But she couldn't do that without worrying that she was making a mistake. "We are good together, and we've accomplished a lot in the past few months, but is that enough to sustain a relationship like marriage? This would be a huge step for both of us. I don't want to fail at another relationship, especially one that would affect my baby and the way we get on so well together here."

"Sarah, what are you so afraid of? Do you think that I would ever abandon you the way Kevan did? Do you think it matters to me whether your baby is mine by blood? The fact that this baby is yours is all I need. I will love and care for both of you if you'll let me."

"I'm afraid that you would come to regret marrying me when you realize my baby will come first. I know this is not what you want to hear, but I already love this child," she said, afraid she had hurt his feelings. "I have to be honest with you."

He came around the corner of the booth and sat beside her, putting his arms around her as he kissed her forehead and smoothed the hair from her face. "I will always be there for you. I told you that months ago. And it's still true. The question is, how do you feel about me?"

She wanted to curl up in his arms, and never think about anything ever again. She was so tired of being responsible, of feeling like she was making a mistake in not putting her child up for adoption. As much as she believed she knew the man whose arms offered such security, she wasn't sure he understood how his life would change when her baby was born.

And how could he take her on, knowing she loved someone else?

"I care a great deal for you. Enough that I don't want you to take on something as complicated as me. Isn't it enough that we are working together, spending our evenings here in this restaurant surrounded by people we know?"

Ben held her, his scent surrounding her, while her ability to resist what he was offering slowly slipped from her in the face of how she felt in that moment. She looked into his eyes, and saw the love shining there.

"Benjamin, I care for you so much. I want us to have a life together, but I need to take it slow, to be sure. I would never be able to forgive myself if I hurt you. You deserve to be happy."

"I am happy right here with you."

BENJAMIN HELD HER CLOSE, the diamond ring he'd purchased secure in his pocket. He'd been so sure that Sarah wanted what he wanted. He'd known for a while she cared for him, relied on him to be there for her. And he had cared, in every way possible, except the one way that mattered most to him. He would give her everything he had or would ever have if she would only agree to marry him.

But he wouldn't tell her that. He would never try to bribe her, or do anything that would make her feel she was being pushed to make a decision. He had all the time in the world to win her over. At least now she knew his intentions.

"Being happy with you will always be true for me," he said, feeling the warmth of her body next to his in the narrow space of the booth.

"I don't know what to say," Sarah whispered, her eyes on his.

He loved these moments when she was totally focused on him. "Why don't I tell you how I feel?"

She smiled that knowing smile of hers. "I'm listening."

"When we first met I had trouble sharing my feelings. I had grown up keeping my feelings to myself. It came mostly from my father, a man who seldom showed any emotion. He'd often caution me about going 'all soft and touchy feely about things' as he liked to call it. He prided himself on being a man who held his cards close to his chest."

He twined his big fingers with her smaller ones. "Like my father, I really believed that as long as I did my job, made money, supported my family, my mother and sister in whatever way I could, I was doing what was expected of me. My feelings would be evident in my actions."

"I remember you telling me that," she said, relaxing against his shoulder.

"Then as I got to know you I realized that I wanted to share things with you. I wanted us to be close. And when I did tell you things, you understood so well what I was saying. I've never confided in anyone the way I have with you. That's how I knew that you and I were meant to be together. No two people can be this close and not love each other. Love is a verb, an action."

"Where did that come from? Love is action?" she asked, smiling up into his face. He wanted to kiss her right then and there, but he needed to tell her what he was feeling before he lost his nerve.

"Probably something Lilly sent me to read. But I truly believe that if you love someone you will do what it takes to make them happy. Making you happy has been important to me since you came here. As for my sister, she's always tried to get me married off," he said ruefully.

"Will she be happy with your proposal to me?"

"She will be delighted." He wasn't sure how his sister would feel, but he didn't care. As for his mother, he knew she would never approve of anyone other than the girl he dated in high school, a long time ago.

"But what I want you to know is that I will wait for you until you're ready to say yes." He eased away from her, fingering the jewel box in his pocket as he did so.

He had to believe that someday she would say yes to him, and her "I do" would make his life complete.

CHAPTER TWENTY-SIX

The next week Sarah came home from running errands to find her mother and father at the house waiting for her.

"This is a surprise," she said, putting her parcels on the kitchen counter. "I thought you weren't arriving until Thanksgiving," she said, her gaze going from one to the other.

Her father shuffled his feet a little, glancing sideways at her mother. "We're here to tell you that we want you to give up your baby. I know we've said all this before, but you haven't listened and we're worried that you'll put off making your decision until it's too late."

She looked at the two people who had held sway over her life for so many years, and realized something. She was not just their daughter anymore. She was a person in her own right, a person who had earned the right to a life of her choosing. As much as she loved them, she had to find a way to explain her life and her choices.

"Mom and Dad, please listen to me. I am not giving away my baby. Ever. And I am so disappointed that you still want me to do something I've said from the beginning I wouldn't do." Sarah took a deep breath. "Please sit down while I tell you what I should have told you months ago."

They sat on either side of her at the table, exchanging anxious glances.

"For the last time, I'm not giving up my baby and I'm not moving back home. My life is here. I'm happy and I want you to be happy for me. This baby will be your grandchild. And if I have to give the baby up, you'll never have a chance to be part of my baby's life. Do you see how impossible this is?" she asked.

"Yes. Of course," her dad said.

"When *this* baby is born, you will be grandparents to a boy or girl who will be part of your life forever."

Her mother's sobs filled the room, body-shaking sobs that frightened Sarah. She had never heard her mother cry like that. How she wished Benjamin was with her. She needed his calm approach. "Mom, I'm sorry if I've hurt you. Truly sorry. But you wouldn't listen."

Her mother wiped the tears from her cheeks, as she continued to cry.

Her father reached across the table. "Doris, please don't cry. We can work this out. I think Sarah has made it clear how she feels. As for me, I can't do this any longer. Maybe this isn't the best way to become grandparents, but I'll take it. I want to be a grandfather. You do too. Can we try to see this from Sarah's point of view?"

"I'm so sorry for what I've put you through. It was wrong. You've proven you can manage," her mother said. "I should have looked at this differently. Been more understanding."

Sarah hugged her mother. "I love you, Mom. And my baby will love you too. We're my baby's family now. We are in this together." An idea came to her. And we can go shopping for baby things together, can't we, Mom?"

"Yes. I would love that. We'll get Elsie to go with us."

"And guess what? I'm moving into the apartment next week

after the kitchen cupboards are installed. Want to see where my baby and I will be living?"

They nodded and rose.

"Follow me," she said, leading them through the connecting link to the apartment. She showed them around the living space before taking them to the bedroom she planned to use as a nursery. "I picked yellow for this room because I don't know if I'm having a boy or a girl." She pointed to the bassinet in the corner. "My friend Leslie Anne and I found this at the local antique dealer's. Don't you love it? I made the padded liner, and Elsie knit a blanket for the baby."

"I can knit too. I'll buy yarn and start knitting baby things as soon as I get home," her mother said. She hugged Sarah. "This is so exciting. I'm so glad we came here today."

"I am too, Mom." As she looked at her parents, at the love in their eyes, she wanted more than anything for them to meet Benjamin. They needed to know that without his help and support she wouldn't have been able to say and believe what she had just said.

When Sarah went into work that evening she told Benjamin about her parents' visit and how they'd worked out their differences over her baby. He was delighted for her, giving her all sorts of encouragement for how she'd handled the situation. It made her feel good to hear him offer words of praise.

TWO DAYS LATER, with a few business issues settled, Benjamin called his mother to say he was coming over with news. He wanted his mom to know all about Sarah and how happy he was. When he got to the door his mother stood there with flour on her apron and a smile on her face.

"Come on in, dear. I see so little of you these days with all your work and the demands on your time." She hugged him close, the scent of rosewater wafting around him.

"I'm glad to be here, Mom. I've missed you. What are you baking?" He linked arms with her as they headed to the kitchen.

"I'm making Hello Dolly squares for my church group tonight, and chocolate chip cookies for the bake sale tomorrow."

"You're busy." He turned to his sister, pulling her into a bear hug. "And what is my dear sister doing?" he asked, as they entered the sun-lit kitchen.

"I'm helping her with the baking."

"Any news on your divorce?"

"Not yet. We're still arguing over support payments."

"This is so hard on you, dear," her mother said as she put the kettle on to boil. "Everyone wants tea, right?"

They nodded together and stood watching their mother put the kettle on. "Where is Timothy, by the way?" Benjamin asked.

"He's at the kindergarten you recommended."

"And have you contacted the hospital about a nursing job, or are you still waiting for your divorce to be final?"

"I put in an application, but nothing yet, other than a night shift," she said, wrinkling her nose.

They settled around the table, as Benjamin searched for a way to broach the subject of his proposal to Sarah. "I have something I need to talk about with both of you," he said.

His mother frowned. "Not business problems, I hope."

"No. Business is good. This is personal."

"About someone you've been seeing? I'm hoping she's the someone I've already met." Lilly said, an impish grin on her face.

"As a matter of fact, it is. Mom, she works in the restaurant. She's also an interior decorator and has done a great job fixing up the restaurant."

"It's Sarah Maddison, isn't it?" Lilly said, turning to her mother. "Mom, you'll really like her. She's sweet. We went shopping for fabric together. We didn't buy anything, but she has a good eye for color and design."

"I saw how nice the restaurant looks. I was there for lunch a few weeks back," his mother said. "How long have you known her? Where is she from?"

"She's been working with me for nearly four months. She's from the Boston area. We have spent a lot of time together. I've come to rely on her for advice and support."

"When will I get to meet her?" his mother asked, hesitantly.

"Soon. Real soon."

"Are you sure about this, dear? You've been a bachelor for a long time. You're very busy with your work. This will be a big change in your life," his mother said, her tone one of caution.

"I am, Mom. I've never been surer about anything in my life."

Eleanor touched his arm. "Then, I'm happy for you. So happy."

"There's something else you need to know about Sarah."

"What's that?" his mother asked, her eyes focused on him in that way of hers that he remembered well.

"Mom, I asked Sarah to marry me."

"What? So soon, dear? You've hardly had time to get to know her, or anything about her."

He wanted to put off telling his mother about the baby, but she deserved to know everything. "Sarah is expecting a baby in a few months."

"She's *what?*" His mother and Lilly cried out in unison.

"Is it yours?" his mother asked, a look of disbelief on her face.

"No. The father is out of her life, and she moved here to have her baby."

"How do you know the father is out of her life?" his mother said, her expression tense. "You only met her a few months ago, and this is so sudden."

"Mom, I love this woman. I trust her completely. She means the world to me. I want you to be happy for me and for her. You will see how special she is when you meet her."

"When will that be?" his mother asked, her eyes watering.

"It will be very soon, I promise. I know this is not what you expected, and I understand your concern, Mom. But Sarah is wonderful. I love her. We will be happy together."

His mother looked at him, and he saw the love in her eyes. "I think you're rushing this, but if she makes you happy..."

Relieved, he hugged her close. "Thanks Mom. You're the best. I have to go away for a couple of days. Why don't we have dinner together when I get back?"

"Here at the house would be best," his mother said, as she exchanged glances with Lilly.

CHAPTER TWENTY-SEVEN

Sarah was so excited as she waited at the bus stop for Cindy. She'd heard from Benjamin twice a day since he'd been away, but his calls only made her more lonesome for him.

Over recent weeks, her feelings for Kevan had changed. She wasn't sure how she felt about him anymore. She had loved him so much, but without him she'd had to face her life on her own. With Benjamin's proposal and his acceptance of her pregnancy she had a chance at a new life with a man who loved and cared for her.

When the bus pulled in, Cindy was the first person out the door, waving her arms in excitement. Rushing to Sarah she threw open her arms. "I have missed you so much, and I have so much to tell you. You're going to be so pleased."

Was her news about Kevan?

Sarah felt a tiny pang of disquiet…

"I'm so glad you're here," she said, hugging Cindy.

"Me too," Cindy said, a wide grin wreathing her face. "I can't believe this is happening."

They held each other for a few minutes, minutes in which Sarah wished that Benjamin was there with her. She wanted him to meet her best friend.

Jostled by the other passengers, Cindy grabbed her suitcase from the ones being unloaded from the bus. "Where do we go from here?"

"My car awaits you, madam," Sarah said, falling back into the old banter they'd always shared.

"You have a car?" Cindy asked. "How grand we are."

They kidded each other all the way home to Sarah's place. "My aunt and uncle turned part of their house into an apartment for me and my baby. It's really sweet. Just the right size for us."

"That so generous of them. And look at you. You look fantastic," Cindy said, patting Sarah's arm as she drove through the streets leading from the bus stop. "And when am I going to see where you work?"

"We'll do that tonight. I want you to come in to work with me for a few hours to see what I'm doing, and why I love it so much," Sarah said, feeling more than happy to have her friend with her.

When they got to the apartment her Aunt Elsie was waiting. "So, this is the friend you've talked about," Elsie said, extending her hand to Cindy. "I've made tea and fresh scones. I'll bring a tray to the apartment so the two of you can settle in and chat. If you like I can make supper as well."

"The tea and scones are more than enough. As for dinner, I have to work this evening as Benjamin isn't back yet," Sarah said.

"And I'm going in with her. I want to learn all about her life here in Bar Harbor. Maybe we can have dinner another time?" Cindy asked.

"Another time will work. I'll be over with the tray in a few minutes."

Once inside the apartment Sarah showed Cindy to the bedroom. "This will be the nursery. My Uncle Fred put a foldaway bed in here for you. I hope it's comfortable."

"I'm sure it will be," Cindy said, glancing around. "What a lovely room. Perfect for a baby."

"If you need to unpack anything..."

"Me? No. Jeans and sweaters are all I have with me, and they don't need to be hung up." Cindy glanced around at the room with its white, lace-edged curtains and the soft yellow walls. "Do you know if it's a boy or a girl?" she asked as they went back to the living room.

"No, and it doesn't matter as long as it's healthy," Sarah said, feeling relaxed for the first time since Benjamin left.

"This is so nice," Cindy said. "I envy you in a way."

"And I envied you. When I first got here, all I could think about was that I wanted to be at college, studying, finding new friends, spending time with you."

"And now all of that has changed?" Cindy asked.

Sarah looked around at her new home, remembering her job and the friends she'd made... Her thoughts rushed to Benjamin and what he might be doing right now... "Yes, it has. I like my life. It's not what I planned, but it's good all the same."

Cindy looked uncertain for the first time ever in Sarah's experience. "I... I'm not doing well in college. I was so sure that being a physiotherapist was what I wanted, but now I'm not so sure. I feel as if life is passing me by—"

They were interrupted by Elsie who smiled apologetically as she put the tray on the coffee table. "I won't bother you girls. Enjoy," she said, leaving as quickly as she'd arrived.

Sarah watched her friend's gaze move around the room.

"Do you like what I've done with the space? I found these chairs in a thrift store, made these pale green cushions for them, and painted the walls cream to go with them. Then I helped pick out the counter tops. Uncle Fred was so pleased to have my advice on color and types of flooring and all that." Glancing over at Cindy, she'd expected to find her enthusiastically following her explanation, but her friend looked lost.

"What's wrong Cindy?"

"You've made a life without Kevan. You haven't asked me what I learned about Kevan's whereabouts. Are you not in love with him anymore?"

She wanted to share her feelings with Cindy, but she wasn't sure what they were. Only recently she'd stopped dreaming about Kevan... He didn't pop into her thoughts the way he had when she first moved to Bar Harbor.

"I guess time has changed some things. In the early weeks after I moved here I went to bed crying for Kevan, and woke up wondering how I would get through the day without him. But as the weeks turned into months, and no one could or would tell me how to reach him, I guess I started to give up."

Sarah poured two cups of tea and passed one to Cindy. "There have been people in my life here who have helped me, and I've come to rely on them."

"Your aunt and uncle, for sure. Who else?" Cindy asked.

"I met a woman at work. Leslie Anne Taylor. You'll meet her tonight when we go in. She has been so helpful, and she has a four-year-old son that she's raising on her own after her husband died. And Benjamin Patterson has helped me so much. I couldn't have made it through these past few months if it hadn't been for him. He owns the restaurant where I work."

"Oh. How involved are you with him? Is he the reason you haven't asked me anything about Kevan?"

"I want to know about Kevan. Anything you can tell me. I want Kevan to know about the baby, and if he's going to be home at Christmas. I need to talk to him," she said.

Cindy shook her head slowly. "I was basically told to get lost when I called the McElroy home. Dad says that no one talks about Kevan anymore. It's as if he vanished in Europe."

"That can't be. Someone has to know what's going on."

"If they do, they are not telling," Cindy said, a note of finality in her voice.

Sarah waited for the pain of loss that always accompanied any mention of Kevan. But there wasn't any. Only a sadness for what might have been.

"Dad says the McElroy family is going to Ireland for Christmas. It's really odd. They never go away at Christmas."

"I talked to Julia and got nothing, but I could try again. Surely by now she's not being grounded," Sarah said.

"Why don't I try for you? I know Julia a little better than you do. She might tell me something, especially if she's getting ready to head out of the country for Christmas. If I get in touch with her, do you want me to pass along your phone number?"

Why didn't she feel more enthusiastic about Cindy's offer? "Sure. If she's willing to take it." Pouring more tea for each of them, Sarah said, brightly, "When we finish here I'll take you into work. It's a busy place, and with Benjamin away I'll be on the go all evening. But I'd like you to stay and meet my friends. Maybe I'll put you to work clearing tables," she said, kidding.

"I'd really like that, Sarah. Honestly, I would love to work where you work. I need to feel as if I'm doing something purposeful, not wasting away in a classroom. And I want us to be close again, the way we were in high school."

"I want that too," she said, acutely aware that in order to be close, she would have to share her feelings about Benjamin.

CHAPTER TWENTY-EIGHT

Once they reached the restaurant, Sarah introduced Cindy to the staff working that evening. Cindy worked along with Sarah, helped clear tables, all the while smiling and laughing with patrons. Sarah was pleasantly surprised to discover that Cindy was a very hard worker. "I'm really proud of you," she said to her friend when they ended up back near the bar.

"I'm proud of me too," Cindy said, glancing around, a triumphant look on her face.

Sarah turned to answer a question from the bartender. He wanted to know if they should order more wine the next day as the inventory was low due to a retirement dinner last evening. "I think we should. I'll look after it tomorrow."

"No." Benjamin said his voice soft and gentle in her ears. "I'll do it. I'm back now and I will look after it. You, my dear, need a day off."

Filled with unexpected joy she turned quickly and looked up into his face. All she could think about was that he was here with her. "You're back early," she said, wrapping her arms around his neck, hugging him close, breathing in his scent, her world righting itself after two days without him.

"I missed you," she said.

"I missed you, too," he said, his strong arms holding her tight.

"Ah… This must be Benjamin," Cindy said, raising her voice over the sudden laughter of a group standing on the other side of the bar.

Sarah pulled away, embarrassed that her friend had seen them embrace. The whole restaurant had seen them embrace. "I'm sorry. Cindy, this is my boss, Benjamin Patterson."

"I've heard a lot about you," Benjamin said, his arm still around Sarah's shoulders. "Welcome to Pattersons' Steak and Seafood Restaurant."

"I'm glad to be here," Cindy said, her eyes moving from Benjamin to Sarah. "You two have become really close friends," she said, with just a hint of unease in her voice.

"If I have my way it will be a whole lot more," Benjamin said, squeezing Sarah closer.

Wanting to distract Cindy from asking questions, Sarah said, "Cindy has worked all evening with me. And if she wasn't going back to college I would hire her to work with us."

Cindy smiled and extended her hand to Benjamin. "Watch out. I could end up here. I'm serious. I may look at a career change."

Benjamin shook her hand, his smile open. "You can come to work here any time you like," he said.

Sarah could see that Cindy was impressed with Benjamin by the way she smiled at him. "And I just may take you up on that."

Benjamin looked down into Sarah's face, his eyes searching hers, his smile holding her captive. "I need to do a couple of things in the office, but I'll be back. Let's plan to have supper here when the shift ends. I'm sure Cindy would like that."

"She would," Sarah said, relaxing a bit and content and happy to have Benjamin back with her.

Benjamin turned his attention to Cindy. "It's great to meet Sarah's best friend. We'll talk a little later, and I hope you'll have supper with us," he said.

"I certainly will," Cindy answered, but her eyes never left Sarah's face.

When Benjamin moved away toward the back of the restaurant, Cindy turned to Sarah. "You do know that man is in love with you," she said.

Sarah took a deep breath, willing for Cindy to understand. "He's asked me to marry him."

"He's *what*? When did you plan to tell me that?"

"I haven't told anyone. I can hardly believe it myself. We've been working together for months, and we get along really well, and he's helped me so much—"

"Have you given him your answer?"

"I want to talk to Kevan first. I need to know if he's coming home. If he's not..."

"Sarah, you can't decide whether or not you'd marry this man based on whether or not you know what Kevan is doing. Either you love this man enough to be his wife, or you don't. It's as simple as that."

"No. It's not that simple. Benjamin is a kind and caring man, and he wants the best for me. He's accepted the fact that I'm expecting a baby, and he supports me in whatever I need to do. And that would mean knowing where Kevan is and being able to tell him about our baby."

Cindy shook her head slowly. "If you're going to marry this man I really feel you need to forget about Kevan. His family is keeping his life and his whereabouts a secret. I saw his best friend from high school when I got back home last week. And he has not heard a word from Kevan either."

Sarah felt the hope she'd been harboring all these months shrivel inside her. "Then he really doesn't want anyone to know where he is."

Cindy glanced around, a tiny frown line forming between her eyes. "I don't know what to tell you. I really wish that Kevan would be in touch with someone."

"Me too. But I can't go on like this. Benjamin deserves a good life, and so do I. I care very much for Benjamin and he loves me, and has since we met."

"That is so sweet," Cindy said. "Wish a man like that would come into my life."

"He will. You will meet the right man, and be really happy. Just like me," Sarah said, feeling generous, wanting everyone to have someone like Benjamin to rely upon.

CHAPTER TWENTY-NINE

Slowly patrons cleared out of the restaurant, leaving Cindy, Sarah and Benjamin to close up. Sarah loved this moment of the day – the tranquility, the peacefulness of the time she'd have with the man who had asked her to marry him.

"I'm so glad you're here with us," Sarah said as she refreshed the white table cloth at their favorite booth. "You'll really enjoy talking with Benjamin. He's so interesting."

"And what else is he?" Cindy asked, arching her eyebrows as she placed three napkins on the table with forks and knives. "Sexy? Fun? Loving? Have you done the deed yet?"

"What? *No!*"

"Well, you can't put it off forever. You do realize that sex will be part of this."

She hadn't thought very much about that. Being pregnant made her feel uneasy about the physical side of their relationship. And Benjamin had never pressured her into having sex with him. "Of course."

"Then tell me about him. How does he make you feel?"

Caught off guard she stared at her friend. "He makes me feel...great."

"Is that all?"

"What do you mean, for heaven's sake. For your information this is not like Kevan and me."

"How is it different?"

"Kevan and I, we were..."

"You were what? Crazy in love? And now you're not? Tell me, Sarah. What's different with Benjamin?"

"You're not being fair. You can't possibility understand what Benjamin has meant to me these past months, and I resent you making it sound like I would marry him without loving him."

Cindy reached out to her. "I want you to be happy. But I don't want you to jump into a new relationship if you aren't over Kevan. Are you over him?"

"Cindy, I've faced months without Kevan. He hasn't contacted me. The simple truth is that if he wanted to be in touch with me he'd have found a way. I'm living here now and I love it. This is where I belong. This is my decision."

"Whose decision are we talking about?" Benjamin asked as he walked up behind her, his hand moving over her back. "How are you doing this evening?" he asked, his lips close to her ear, sending chills of delight down her spine.

SEEING the anxiety in Sarah's eyes, Benjamin resisted the urge to wrap his arms around her. He sensed that she and her friend had been arguing about something, and he had a pretty good idea what that was.

"Cindy, I had the cook leave a crown roast and vegetables for us this evening. I hope you like pork."

"I love it," Cindy said, her tense expression easing as she met his gaze.

He liked this young woman, but he would not allow her to upset Sarah in her delicate condition. He'd come home prepared to have a beautiful dinner with Sarah, had even called ahead to have the roast prepared in advance so he could give Sarah the ring he'd been carrying around with him for weeks. "Then, we'll have a delicious meal while we talk about our day," he said, once again his eyes going to Sarah and noting the tense set of her shoulders.

She smiled at him and he realized again, after being away from her, that a smile from her could light up his life. He felt good that he'd talked to his mother about his plan to marry this woman. His sister, Lilly, and mother had expressed surprise. Yet, they both seemed to understand how he felt, and when they expressed their concern about his haste, he understood it but was not swayed.

The real shock had come when he'd told them Sarah was expecting. At first they'd assumed it was his baby, and looking back he wished he'd lied and said it was his. But he hadn't. And this was his life. He'd waited a long time for a woman like Sarah, and he wasn't about to give her up.

He welcomed the arrival of the cook with their meal. It provided an opportunity to find out what was going on between Sarah and her best friend. "Let's eat before it gets cold," he said, his hand on Sarah's back as he helped ease her into the seat, noting that the space between her tummy and the table was getting smaller. "Starting next week, we're going to set up a table at the back of the restaurant, more intimate and out of the way. What do you think, Sarah?"

"Either that, or we make the booth bigger," she said, her eyes shining with humor.

He settled in beside her, facing Cindy, and served the plates of food to each of them, fully aware Cindy was watching him closely.

"How did your meetings go?" Sarah asked as she picked up her fork and began to eat.

Benjamin was secretly pleased to see how much Sarah enjoyed

food. He'd always been a little resentful of the women he dated who proclaimed their lack of interest in food when he was in the food business. It always felt like some sort of veiled criticism.

Reaching under the table he squeezed Sarah's hand. "The meetings were great. I'm thinking about buying a property near the highway that I can have as a gas station and variety store for people traveling on the Interstate," he said by way of explanation for Cindy as Sarah already knew why he'd been away.

"You are really busy," Cindy said. "Is it always like this?" she asked glancing around the now dimly lit restaurant.

"Some days it's even busier," Sarah said, her voice radiating pride as she squeezed his hand.

They ate in silence for a few minutes, then Cindy excused herself to go to the restroom.

Taking advantage of the few moments they had alone, he said, "So you told Cindy we're getting married?"

"Yes, I did."

"What did she say?" he asked, sensing that what he'd witnessed earlier between the two women was all about his proposal.

Sarah sighed. "Cindy thinks I'm rushing things."

His heart lurched. "Do you feel the same way?"

She turned to him, giving him the full benefit of her smile. "She's worried that since I can't find Kevan, I'm not being fair. I told her I've done everything I can to find him, to tell him about the baby. I can't continue living with the hope that he will show up in Boston with an explanation of where he's been and what is going on."

He'd done his own search, looking for Kevan McElroy, but had hit a brick wall. Even so, that wouldn't stop him from continuing his search for the man who had abandoned the woman he loved. He believed that once she realized how happy they were together with her baby, that if Kevan returned looking for Sarah, she would not care one way or the other about him.

"Sarah, I promise you that if he should ever show up we will deal with it. He will be a father, but not a parent. I will be your baby's dad. I've told you I would, and I mean it."

She gave a murmured cry, her arms circling his neck. "Thank you. I can't believe how lucky I am to have you in my life."

"Sarah, this isn't how I intended to do this, but..." He reached into the pocket of his sports jacket and took out the small black leather box. "I can't wait to marry you." He opened the box and held it out to her.

"It's beautiful!" she gasped, her fingers fluttering over the velvet lining of the box, touching the square cut diamond nestled there.

He took it out and slid it on her finger. "I love you," he said, his heart rising in his throat at the thought of what the future held with the woman who meant everything to him.

Sarah held up her hand, her face wreathed in a huge smile. "I love you, too."

He pulled her into his arms, kissing her, his hands moving over her back, her body pressed to his. "I have never been this happy in my entire life," he whispered into her neck as he kissed her. "Sarah, I wake up every morning and my first thought is you."

"Me too.... I feel so good about all of it." She glanced at her finger. "And this ring is so beautiful."

"Then we need to set a date. How about Christmas?" he asked, imagining the snow-covered inn he'd discovered in Vermont. He'd seen photos of the place in a travel magazine while waiting for one of his meetings the day before.

She stared at him wide-eyed. "A Christmas wedding?"

"Or any time in the next few months."

"You want to marry a pregnant woman?"

"What other woman would I want to marry?" he asked enjoying the look of awe mingled with happiness on her face. "If I had my way we would be married tomorrow."

"You mean it?" The look of happiness on Sarah's face filled him with joy.

"Absolutely. Just say the word and I'll marry you."

"Well, what have we here?" Cindy said in a joking tone as she approached the table.

Sarah tensed in his arms. He'd been right. Sarah was worried about what her friend thought of her new-found happiness...

"You are looking at the two of the happiest people in the world," he said, his arms holding Sarah close as he smiled at her friend.

"Look at this." Sarah held her hand out, her laughter of delight the happiest sound he'd ever heard.

"OH! I am so happy for both of you. Congratulations." Cindy reached across the table to take hold of Sarah's left hand. "That is gorgeous," she breathed, turning Sarah's fingers so the light glinted off the large diamond. "I suppose it's too early to ask when you're planning to be married?"

Sarah's heart pounded so hard she could barely breathe. She turned to Benjamin whose eyes met hers, and a smile formed on his lips. "We...haven't had time to really decide about that. There is so much to think about."

"Your mom and dad will be pleased, won't they?"

"I think they will be really happy for me. For us." She continued to meet Benjamin's loving gaze, remembering how only a while ago she had had no idea he felt like this about her.

Benjamin turned from her, his gaze focused on Cindy. "We haven't worked any of the details out. All I know for sure is that I want to marry Sarah as soon as possible."

Cindy's lips moved as if she were going to say something. Sarah was pretty sure she knew what was on her friend's mind.

"Cindy, Benjamin knows all about Kevan. He and I have agreed that when Kevan is found he will be told about the baby."

Benjamin hugged her tight, his hand covering the ring he'd just given her. "We would never deny him the right to see his child."

"You're two very brave people," Cindy said.

"What do you mean by that?" Benjamin asked.

"Tom McElroy is a hard man. He may have something to say when he learns he has a grandson."

Benjamin searched her face. "We don't have to worry about anyone interfering with this baby. Sarah will know every moment of happiness as my wife and as a mother. I'll see to it."

Sarah looked into his eyes, feeling the strength behind his words. And in that instant, she felt completely safe and protected.

This man would care for her and her baby, no matter what.

The thought warmed her, making her feel like the most special woman in the whole world.

"Sarah, I am so happy for you. You have found someone who will love you through thick and thin." Cindy brushed the hair off her forehead. "Are there more men around here like Benjamin?" she asked, her voice light, her smile easy.

"I have no idea," Sarah said, reaching up to touch Benjamin's cheek.

Laughing he held her hand up, kissing her ring finger. "I can't wait to tell the whole world about us. We need to think about a date for our wedding."

"Can I help with your wedding plans?" Cindy asked. "I love weddings and parties. Heaven knows I was at enough of them this semester to last me a lifetime. Probably why I did so poorly on my exams."

As Sarah gazed at her friend, she realized how much she wanted Cindy at her wedding, to be part of it. "That would be great. You can be my maid-of-honor."

"I would be delighted," Cindy said, a huge grin on her face.

"Then it's settled. Once we set a date you two can start planning," Benjamin said, his eyes focused solely on Sarah.

She snuggled closer to him as they sat across from her best friend. "Everything is going to be perfect."

"Well, then, we'd better finish our meal and get a little rest. It sure sounds like we're going to be busy," Benjamin said, glancing from one to the other, before kissing her.

THE NEXT MORNING, Sarah told her aunt and uncle who danced around the kitchen in excitement. She called her parents and her mother sobbed on the phone, going on about how wonderful Benjamin was. That he was the answer to her prayers. Sarah loved seeing the people she loved so happy. And all because of Benjamin.

In the middle of it all, Cindy announced she was leaving university and moving to Bar Harbor. She wanted to be with Sarah, to share her excitement. Sarah couldn't believe her good fortune. In less than a day her life had changed completely.

CHAPTER THIRTY

A few days later, days filled with early morning chats after long nights in the restaurant, a trip to finish up one of Sarah's decorating jobs, followed by hours of combing through bridal magazines, and Sarah was exhausted but happy.

They were driving back from the restaurant late one evening when Cindy asked, "Don't you *ever* go home with Benjamin after work?"

"No."

"Why not?"

Sarah didn't know why not. They'd never talked about her going to his place. She'd been inside his house once when he had to pick something up on his way to work. "Because we don't want to."

"Don't want to do what? It's not like you're a virgin," Cindy said, turning to face Sarah.

"Cindy, please don't talk like that. I am well aware that I've gone to bed with someone." She looked down at her belly for emphasis. "But Benjamin and I want to wait until we're married. We want to do things the right way."

"Sarah, it's me you're talking to. Remember?"

"I... I can't face the idea that people will talk about how I'm expecting a baby and sleeping with my boss."

Cindy sighed. "I'm sorry for being so blunt. I keep forgetting how many months you've been here, and what you must have gone through."

"It's okay. We are all living differently than we planned. How's the job, by the way?"

"That man of yours is so kind. He mentioned to me last night that there might be a position managing one of his apartment buildings. It would mean that I'd have my own apartment as part of the deal. Isn't that great?"

"It is. And it's so like Benjamin, doing the right thing by people he cares about."

"I can't imagine why some woman hadn't snapped him up a long time ago."

Sarah considered the idea. "You know, I've secretly wondered about why he isn't already married, but he told me that he just knew I was the one. It's so romantic."

"Then, why don't you want to set a date for the wedding?"

"I'm waiting for Mom and Dad to get here."

"But shouldn't you be talking to Benjamin about this first?"

"We talk about it every day. He wants to get married at Christmas at an inn in Vermont."

"I can't imagine a more romantic setting. What do you think?" Cindy asked.

"It would be perfect," Sarah said, smiling at the idea of a beautiful Christmas wedding in the mountains of Vermont.

"If I were you, I would tell him you'll marry him at Christmas. What are you waiting for?"

"I have to meet his mother first."

"You haven't met her?" Cindy asked, surprised. "Have you met his sister?"

"Yes. She's really nice. As for his mother, there never seems to be time...and Lilly's divorce has been the focus of Eleanor's life these past months, as I understand it."

"You'd better get on it. You can't get married without meeting the woman."

They drove in silence for a few minutes before Sarah brought up the subject. "Cindy, I realize that I probably shouldn't even be talking about this right now, given how great my life is. But I would still like to find Kevan and tell him he's going to be a dad before—"

"Sarah, when I came here I was really upset with you, that you seemed to have forgotten about Kevan. But now that I see your life, the man you're going to marry, and your fabulous chance at happiness, I think you need to wake up to the fact that your relationship with Kevan is over. My advice is marry Benjamin, have your baby and be happy."

"You're right. It's probably just pre-wedding jitters." Sarah drove into the driveway, shut off the engine and got out. "You're right about a whole lot of things. I'm going to call Benjamin. Tell him I'm coming over to his house and we'll set the date."

Cindy gave a whoop of joy. "You do that. And don't come back here until you can tell me when I'm going to perform my duties as maid-of-honor."

Sarah went in and called Benjamin. He answered on the first ring, his voice sounding tired. "Did I wake you?" she asked.

"No. I'm glad to hear your voice. Is there something wrong? You're not in labor, are you?"

"No. I thought I'd drop over and we could get out the calendar and set the date."

There was a long sigh of relief on the other end of the phone. "I've already marked every Saturday in December off for me, just so that I can be ready to marry you. Come on over here, and we'll set the date."

"I'll be there as soon as I can."

"I'll have the porch light on. Drive carefully."

Sarah drove as quickly as she could toward Benjamin's end of town, making one wrong turn before she found his house on a quiet cul-de-sac. Once in the driveway, she got out of the car to see Benjamin coming down the walkway, his arms out in welcome.

"I'm so glad you're here. Don't mind the mess in the kitchen," he said. "The cleaning lady doesn't come until tomorrow, and I wanted her to have something to do," he kidded, his arm around her shoulders as he guided her up the steps into the foyer.

He took her jacket and hung it up, turning her in his arms. "I can't wait to have you here redecorating this place while I watch and enjoy every second of it." He kissed her, his lips a gentle caress. He ran his hands over her shoulders, making her body tingle. "I love you, soon-to-be Mrs. Benjamin Patterson."

"I love you too," she whispered, running her hands through his hair, kissing his jawline, soaking in the warmth of his touch, his scent, all those things she'd come to love about him. So many things.

He held her away from him, his eyes searching hers. "When you called I had just learned something that might affect our future. I need to talk to you."

The dark expression on his face scared her. *Was he ill? Had he had a serious business setback? Had he changed his mind about marrying her?*

"What is it?" she asked, as a slow tremble started in her core. *He couldn't have changed his mind, could he?* And yet the look in his eyes...

Taking her hand in his, he led her toward the sofa in the living room. "Let's sit down while we talk."

She looked into his eyes, dark with anxiety.

"Please Benjamin. Whatever it is, we will get through this together," she said, taking his hand, holding it tight while she prayed that what he had to say would not change their life, their plans. She couldn't face another loss, just when she had so much to look forward to. As her eyes held his, she tried for a smile, failing miserably. She waited what seemed like a lifetime before he spoke.

BENJAMIN WATCHED HER FACE, trying to crank up the courage to tell her what he'd learned about Kevan's whereabouts. He shouldn't have done what he did. He had no business digging into her past, none at all. Yet as she looked at him with that endearing way of hers, he knew he could never really be happy until he told her the truth.

He cleared his throat, feeling the kind of anxiety that made his stomach ache. "I did something I'm not proud of."

"Oh, Benjamin. That can't be true. You're the best person I know." The look of adoration in her eyes was a look he wanted her to have forever. Surely what he knew could change things... And keeping things the way they were mattered most to him.

And that adoration would disappear if he told her what he knew.

What if he didn't tell her?

They were truly happy, and had so much to look forward to as they planned their wedding. She had been so happy since he'd proposed. How could he say something that would change her, possibly take her happiness from her?

Once they were married he'd make her even happier, and she wouldn't care about what he'd learned. And just because a man fathered a child, didn't mean he had the right to interfere in someone else's happiness.

He'd struggled with this for hours, ever since the phone call he'd received from his contact at the State Department. Maybe she didn't need to know right now. Maybe once the baby was born, and they'd been happy together, he would share what he knew and then they could decide together what would be in the best interests of their baby.

Sarah didn't talk so much about Kevan anymore, and if she could look at him like she was at that moment, it was pretty certain she didn't love Kevan anymore. No, she seldom looked sad and she seldom mentioned Kevan, and he was pretty sure why.

Sarah loved *him*. He saw it in her eyes every time she looked at him. Why tell her something he had no business knowing and ruin their happiness, her happiness?

What should he do?

As he looked into her eyes to the love he saw shining there, he realized there was only one option available to him, to them. Their relationship was based on the truth, and as painful as it might be when he told her what he'd found out, he had to tell her. He had no choice.

Needing to feel her skin on his, he took both her hands, squeezing them gently to reassure himself that he was doing the right thing. "I have to ask you something. It's very important to our future."

Her hands jumped in his. "What? What is wrong, Benjamin? You're scaring me."

He had found Kevan, but he didn't want to tell her. If he did, he could lose her, and he couldn't lose her. "We haven't had this conversation before, but it's important. I need to know how you'd feel if you could see Kevan again?"

SHE DREW IN A DEEP BREATH, her hands holding his tighter as she sorted through her feelings. Those were the last words she'd expected to hear from him. "I...I don't know. Maybe I'd want to... If I could see him, and tell him about the baby."

"And if he wanted to come back into your life? To claim you and your baby after all this time? How would you feel?"

"Benjamin, why are you asking about Kevan? You know everything I know about him, and that's basically nothing. I haven't heard from him since he left." She met his intense gaze, and suddenly wondered. "Do you think I've been talking to him without telling you?" She squeezed his hands. "You must know I wouldn't do that. I have no secrets from you."

He swallowed hard. "We're about to be married and I need to know if you have any doubts about us."

She looked away, her eyes searching the room. *Where was this coming from?*

"Sarah, if you want I could see what I could do to find him."

At his words, her heart trembled in her chest. She knew he would search for Kevan until he found him, if she wanted him to. But would it change how she felt about Benjamin if she were to see Kevan again? Would it end her happiness with the man she was about to marry, or would she see, once and for all, that she had made the right decision in accepting Benjamin's proposal?

She met his gaze, as she pulled her hands from his and touched his cheek. "If I believed that it was possible to see him, it would mean I could tell him about the baby. If I did that, and he came back out of some sort of sense of duty or pity for me…it wouldn't mean anything. Kevan has had months to be in touch with me and he hasn't: that is not what he promised. I have to accept that he's made his plans and they don't include me."

As the words slipped from her lips, she heard the truth of them. She had loved Kevan with all her heart and soul. But it was time to face reality.

She held Benjamin's face in her hands. "I want to marry you and make a life for us. I want to be happy. I cannot wait and wonder about what might have been when I have what I want right here in front of me."

He pulled her into his arms, holding her hard against him, exhaling softly against her cheek. "Thank you, so much. I promise to make you the happiest woman on the planet," he said.

She felt the dampness of tears on her cheek and realized they weren't her tears. The man she loved had been moved to tears.

"I never want you to worry about Kevan, ever again. You and I are going to be married by Christmas. I talked to Mom, told her about our plans. And she wants to meet you."

"If I'm going to be her daughter-in-law, I *should* meet her, Benjamin," she said, giving him a cheeky grin.

"You'll meet her, and you'll love her, just as I do." He picked her up, holding her close as he spun her around, laughing with delight.

She could feel the pounding of his heart through the shirt he wore. She was so thankful that this man loved her the way he did.

CHAPTER THIRTY-ONE

They talked all night, cuddled together on the sofa, told each other every story about growing up they could remember, funny things, sad things, and together they cried tears of joy and of loss. By morning they'd fallen asleep sprawled on the sofa, their arms around each other. When the phone rang, they both leapt up, startled and a little disoriented.

Benjamin answered the phone in the kitchen, his hair disheveled and his shirt half out of his pants. She found him so handsome in his crumpled state. Following him to the kitchen she found the coffee percolator and the coffee, filled the pot with water, spooned in the coffee and put it on the burner to boil. Half listening to his conversation that was clearly about work, she opened the fridge to find milk. She also found a loaf of bread and made toast while she waited for him to finish his conversation.

He placed his hand over the mouthpiece. "What time are we meeting your parents at your aunt and uncle's place?"

"Oh. I nearly forgot!" She checked her watch. "It's almost 9:00. I need to get home."

Benjamin spoke into the phone before ending the conversation.

He went to her, holding her close. "This will be your home in a matter of weeks, my darling."

She snuggled against him as the coffee began to perk and imagined the two of them here with the baby, and a small office space where she could work on her interior decorating commissions. "We will have a wonderful life here," she whispered against his lips as he bent his head down to hers.

After a piece of toast and coffee, Benjamin showered and dressed quickly while Sarah cleaned up the kitchen. He met her at the door his keys in his hands.

"Let's go. Telling your parents about us, and our plans, is a whole new beginning for us." He picked her up and spun her around. "And very soon I'm going to be carrying you over the threshold," his said, his hands firm around her, his eagerness infectious.

THEY ARRIVED at the house in time to see her parents drive up the street behind them.

"They're here," she called out, glancing quickly at Benjamin whose face was wreathed in a smile, one she was pretty sure had been there since they left his house.

Once in the driveway, Sarah got out and went to them. "Mom. Dad. I am so glad you're here," she said, hugging them both, her happiness knowing no bounds at the sight of the two people she had missed so much.

Benjamin followed them into the house where Fred, Elsie and Cindy were waiting. Cindy took her aside, whispering, "You owe me. I've been telling your aunt and uncle you had to leave early, some problem at work. But I think they saw right through my story. I can imagine what's going through their heads." Cindy arched one eyebrow.

"Thanks for trying to help, but it's all okay. Benjamin and I have news." She glanced at each person in turn, her eyes coming to rest on her husband-to-be. "I think you know what I'm about to say." She glanced from her aunt and uncle to her parents. "Benjamin and I are getting married at Christmas." She held out her hand to show them her engagement ring.

Her father's smile of delight swept the room. "Darling girl, we're so happy for you and Benjamin.

"That is the most beautiful diamond I've ever seen," her mother murmured, kissing Sarah on the cheek.

"It is perfect. Everything is perfect," Sarah whispered, happiness washing through her as she hugged her mother. Then she hugged each of them in turn, finding herself in Benjamin's arms at the end of the circle. He cleared his throat nervously at he faced her family around the kitchen table.

"I took a chance and booked the Grey Goose Inn. It's a lovely old place with huge chimneys, lots of brick and the meals are really good. I went there on my way home a few days ago, and decided that if I could, I would convince Sarah to marry me there."

"Are we invited?" Fred asked, to roars of laughter, Sarah's mother laughing the loudest.

"You are all invited. In fact, I tentatively booked rooms for all of us to stay after the wedding. We can have Christmas there. Or I hope we can," he looked momentarily uncertain as his eyes searched Sarah's face.

"That sounds perfect," she said, her heart overflowing with happiness.

"Looks like we don't have much more to do other than show up," her uncle Fred said.

"Hold it." Cindy put her hand up. "There are a few things we need to settle. We will need a wedding dress, a maid-of-honor dress, a new suit for Benjamin, and whoever is going to be his best man."

"I'll offer to be the best man," Fred volunteered.

They all began laughing and talking at once. Sarah looked around at all the people she loved, all the love they gave her, especially Benjamin. "I feel like I'm living in a dream."

"No, darling. It's real. I've been waiting for you for a very long time," he whispered against her ear as he held her in his arms.

"We need to visit your mom right away. I don't want her to feel left out of our happiness."

"Let's do it now. I'll use your aunt's phone and let Lilly and Mom know we're coming over," he said.

"I have to change my clothes and brush my teeth before I can go anywhere. I've been in the outfit all night, remember?"

"I'm not likely to forget."

Sarah leaned closer. "I'm a little nervous."

"Don't be. You and Mom will get along just fine."

When they reached his mother's house, he got out, came around the car and opened the door for Sarah. "Are you ready, darling?"

"As ready as I'll ever be."

They reached the front door and went in. "Hi, Mom. Sarah and I are here."

His mother came down the hall toward him, holding out her arms. "I'm glad to see you, dear," she said as she reached up and hugged him. "Lilly will be down in a few minutes."

She turned to Sarah, her gaze raking over her. "So, this is Sarah," she said, "It's time we met."

Lilly came down the stairs, young Timothy trailing along behind her. "Hi Benjamin. Hi Sarah," she said, smiling as she gave her brother a peck on the cheek.

"Hi Lilly." Sarah knelt down. "Hi Timothy."

He watched her, his eyes wide.

"Mrs. Patterson, I'm so glad to meet you, and I want you to know that I love your son, and I will make him happy," she said, but Benjamin heard the anxiety in her voice.

His mother led Sarah to the living room. "Are you sure, dear, about marrying so soon? Are you doing this because of your baby?"

"No." She glanced at Benjamin, looking for support.

Seeing her need for him, he sat down beside her, taking her hand in his. Turning to his mother who sat down across from them, he said gently. "We might as well discuss this now, get it out in the open. Mom, I realize that what we're doing isn't what you had hoped for, where I'm concerned. But we have a baby arriving in a few months, and I will be its father. I'm fine with that. We'll have more children of our own, but this baby will be special."

"Where is the father?" Eleanor directed her question at Sarah.

"He's out of the country working. He's not involved."

His mother's tense expression told him that she wasn't dealing very well with all this.

"Mom, trust me. We are happy, and we will be happier when this baby arrives. Mom, if it will help you understand I'll come over tomorrow and we'll talk."

His mother sat up straight, gave Sarah one more glance then turned to Benjamin. "I think that would be a good idea. I must apologize. I didn't behave very well. But you took me so by surprise…" Her voice trailed off.

As they left the house, Benjamin hugged Sarah. "I'm sorry. My mom doesn't accept change very easily."

Sarah took his hand in hers. "It's okay. We should have talked to her sooner. It may not have been fair to her. After all, you're her only son."

"I'm glad you are so understanding about this. And you're right. We should have talked to her. I recently told her about you, but I should have talked to her from the first moment I knew how I felt about you. But I will spend time with my mom in the next few weeks, and help her see how much we love each other. I'll take her to Boston to find the perfect mother-of-the-groom dress. Mom loves to shop."

CHAPTER THIRTY-TWO

Grey Goose Inn, Christmas 1976...

*S*arah turned slowly in front of the full-length mirror, the silken folds of her floor-length wedding dress whispering as she moved. "I love this dress," she said, smoothing her fingers over the A-line top that gently disguised her waistline.

Outside the frost-fringed windows, delicate petals of snowflakes fluttered against the glass. The air inside was warm with the scent of cinnamon and evergreen, while the light from the chandelier glinted off the windows beyond the mirror.

Her mother joined her, adjusting her pill box hat that matched her pearl-gray suit. "You look lovely, darling. I'm so happy for you. Benjamin is a good man and you will be very happy." She stroked her daughter's cheek, a smile softening her features.

Her mother touched Sarah's heart-shaped locket. "Darling, you're not going to wear this on your wedding day, are you?" Her mother looked anxious, her fingers working under the gold chain holding the locket around Sarah's neck.

She'd worn the locket so much she felt naked without it. "Oh!

I…Yes. I mean, no. I shouldn't wear it," Sarah said, embarrassed that she hadn't removed the locket before arriving at the inn.

"Why don't I give you these," she said, unclasping the string of pearls from around her neck. "We must remember the old wedding adage: something old, something new, something borrowed, something blue, and a six-pence in your shoe," her mother said, as she waited for Sarah to unfasten the clasp on the chain.

With her fingers trembling slightly, Sarah lifted the locket from her neck.

"That's better, Sarah. You don't want Benjamin to see you wearing that, especially given what you have inside it."

Sarah held the necklace in the palm of her hand, a strange sensation flooding her consciousness. *Where was Kevan? Why hadn't he cared enough to call her during all these months?*

Her mother took her hand and removed the locket, placing it on the dressing table. "Sarah, don't do that to yourself, to Benjamin," her mother cautioned.

"Do what?" Sarah asked, feeling ashamed that she could be thinking of another man on her wedding day.

"Sarah, you have a wonderful husband, a baby just a few months away, and so much to look forward to. Do not let the past ruin what you have." Her mother sighed, a loving smile on her face. "I love you, darling, but you have to move on. Start by putting that locket away…for good."

"You don't have to worry, Mom. I am marrying the man I love, someone I know will stand by me and protect me," she said, forcing her thoughts to the present.

"You are. Now, turn around while I fasten the clasp on these pearls," her mother said.

She felt the coolness of her mother's fingers as she fastened the clasp. "Thanks, Mom."

"You're welcome," her mother hugged her close. "You will be happy with Benjamin."

"Yes, I will, Mom. He and I will be very happy together."

"Just one thing left to do," her mother said, patting Sarah's shoulders affectionately. "The veil," she said, moving to the dressing table where a round box rested. She opened it and lifted the hair combs adorned with white silk roses and tulle netting.

Sarah reached for it and turned to face the mirror again. They both watched her reflection in the mirror as Sarah placed the elegantly decorated combs in her hair.

"Beautiful. You look so beautiful, Sarah," she said.

They were still looking at the image of the two of them in the mirror when Cindy came into the room carrying a nosegay of red roses and baby's breath. Sarah's father walked along behind her, looking proud and happy.

Sarah turned, went to her father and hugged him. "Dad, I'm so glad you're here."

"You are the most beautiful bride in the world," her father said, holding her, kissing her cheek while he touched her shoulders tentatively, as if she might dissolve in his hands.

"Thanks, Dad. And you look great in that tuxedo. I've never seen you wear one before."

"It was Benjamin's idea. He wanted everyone to be dressed up," he said, proudly. "I like that man, Sweet Pea. Really like him."

Cindy linked arms with Sarah. "You are fabulous in that dress. Benjamin is going to flip out when he sees you. The photographer is waiting at the bottom of the stairs. Everyone is downstairs in the main reception room. I introduced myself to Benjamin's mother and sister. Lilly is really funny, and so pretty. Eleanor... I'm not so sure."

"Now, Cindy, no dark thoughts today, of all days," Sarah teased, pulling her friend close.

"Absolutely not," Cindy said, her eyes moving over Sarah. "Okay, final inspection before you go down that dreamy staircase."

Sarah turned slowly one last time, letting the dress move with her, the scent of the roses in her bouquet wafting around her. She looked from Cindy to her parents, all with huge smiles on their faces. They would be there for her wedding, for the arrival of her baby, and for a long time after that. She was happier than she could have imagined.

"This is it. In a few minutes I'll be Mrs. Benjamin Patterson." She reached for her father's arm. "Here we go, Dad."

"The proudest moment of my life," he said as he tucked her hand in the crook of his arm and started toward the door. When they reached the top of the curving staircase, Sarah looked down the length of it to the man standing at the bottom.

Benjamin stood there, looking up at her, his eyes alight with happiness.

"Somebody is waiting just for you, Sweet Pea," her father whispered, a catch in his voice.

"Yes, Dad, someone is." She smiled with gratitude and love at Benjamin as she started down the marble steps.

They walked together, with each step drawing closer to the man she would spend her life with. Sarah's heart flooded with joy.

Once at the bottom, Benjamin reached for her. "You are the most beautiful woman I have ever seen, and in a few minutes, you will be my wife," he said, his voice filled with awe.

"You take it from here, Benjamin, with my blessing," her dad said, shaking Ben's hand before giving Sarah a long, gentle hug. "Love him with all your heart. There is no other way."

Her eyes damp with unshed tears, she took Benjamin's hand and walked with him to the reception hall where the justice of the peace waited near the columned entrance to the patio beyond.

The harpist began "The Wedding March."

"It's here. The moment we've been waiting for," Benjamin said, as he held her hand firmly in his.

Together they crossed the rose petal-covered gold carpet to where the justice of the peace stood.

Sarah glanced back, searching for her mother.

"Be happy," her mother whispered, as she slipped into a chair a few feet away. Her dad moved to stand next to Benjamin.

Cindy reached to take Sarah's bouquet, her eyes teary. "Love you. Enjoy every minute."

Not able to look at Cindy for fear she would cry, Sarah turned to Benjamin.

His eyes were focused solely on her. "This is it. You and me for the rest of our lives," he whispered.

"Are you ready?" the justice of the peace asked.

"We are," Benjamin said, standing tall, still holding her hand in his.

"Ladies and gentlemen, we are gathered here today to celebrate the marriage of Benjamin Andrew Patterson and Sarah Louise Maddison."

THE END

DEAR READER

Young Love is not the whole story of Kevan and Sarah's love for each other.

The second book in the duet, **Of Love and Life**, finds Sarah and Benjamin settling into married life and buying a home along the water outside Bar Harbor. When her son Andrew is born she is alarmed to discover that she experiences the pain of losing Kevan all over again. Yet, life goes along. Andrew is an adorable little boy. Benjamin's business interests are very successful. Everything seems perfect, all but Sarah's sense that life is passing her by. When they don't have another child to complete their family Sarah begins to find a way to express her unhappiness through painting. Her evolution from homemaker to renowned artist, yearning for more in her life than a work-obsessed man who doesn't understand her need to create, leads her to see that the marriage she believed would last a lifetime, would protect and nurture her, is an illusion.

When an act of faith brings Kevan back into her life, she realizes that true love is eternal. An unbreakable bond. That she and Kevan belong together, forever.

This is an excerpt from **Of Love and Life**. It's the first moment when Benjamin and Sarah realize their fundamental difference in how they see life.

~

Andrew wiggled out of his father's arms. "I drew a big elephant," Andrew announced as he led the way upstairs, his feet tapping a happy beat on the wooden treads.

"Daddy, see mine," Andrew demanded, leading his father to the sheet of paper with the bright pink elephant on it.

Benjamin gathered his son in his arms. "That's great, Andrew. Nice and bright. What does Mommy think?" he asked, glancing at her over Andrew's shoulder.

Easing into the room, she offered, "Mommy thinks he has talent," she said, acutely aware that Benjamin was not comfortable in her work space.

"I'll paint some more," Andrew said, wiggling from his father's arms, grabbing the washable marker resting along the edge of the table.

"This is a photo of the painting I sent into the contest. There are parts of it I really like. And other parts I wish I'd done differently. According to Amelia, that's how it works. An artist seldom is totally satisfied with a work. I just hope the judges don't think I'm a total idiot for entering when I've only painted a few pieces." She looked at him, wishing he'd say something.

Benjamin struggled to come up with words to say, partly because he knew nothing about art, and partly because he could see in his wife's eyes her need for him to show his appreciation for her efforts. He focused on the photograph, working on the words he would say. "How big is this?"

"It's about two feet by two feet. I didn't know what size canvas to use, so I went with what was in the art shop."

He could hear the tentative tone in her voice. She was waiting for more from him, more support or interest. All he could think of to say was, "I can't imagine how much work and energy went into this. I had no idea you were doing such impressive work."

She came and stood beside him, taking the photo from his fingers, her touch on his arm reassuring. "I spent hours up here, just getting the basic layout of the painting. I sketched it, and erased it, and sketched it again. It still didn't feel right until I started to work on the canvas. Then it just came together for me."

"How many hours did it take?" he asked, wishing he knew the words that would show that he was knowledgeable about art, and that he could say something that would sound like he knew what he was talking about.

"Oh. Days. Weeks. I don't know." She sighed, as she led him over to the easel. "I've started this one. I love the exquisite beauty of flowers, the petals, the way it makes me feel to take a brush in my hand and let the feeling flow through me; the way color can be shaded, shaped, the imperfection of strokes, yet it all leads somewhere.... It's difficult to describe."

"What is it?" he asked, then wished he hadn't said those words.

An uneasy smile slid across her face. "In this painting I'm working on." She touched the corner of the easel. "I'm trying to do the hedgerow in the back yard, with the delphiniums running along the edge. The many shades of green, the dark of the earth, the blue of the delicate flower, it is all so important. Yet, I don't think I have the right angle."

He couldn't see any of it, only shades of green, and smudged blue with little shape. "Where did you get the idea?" he asked, wanting to leave. It was the hardest conversation he'd had in weeks, even worse than all the talk about his new office building and the planned expansion of Patterson's Restaurant.

"I've been studying the works of the French Impressionists. Amelia and I talk about their art a lot. She knows so much, and she's been so kind."

He watched his wife's face as she spoke, the way her eyes seemed lit by something he couldn't see, something that filled her with energy and enthusiasm.

She looked up into his face. "It's so important to me to be able to paint. Whether I ever exhibit or simply paint for my own pleasure, I have to do it. I don't think I ever told you this, but when I couldn't go to Hastings to take design after high school, I was so disappointed. I felt as if my life was over in a way I couldn't explain to anyone. But maybe it was the best for me. As much as I would have enjoyed design, being able to paint is much more about who I am. My passion." She hugged him, her soft, slightly swollen body pressing into his. "And you made it all possible."

He hadn't intended to make it possible. He'd intended to give her the kind of life where she spent her time and energy on him, their children and on their life together. But the more he thought about it, the more he realized that all of this stuff might be helpful if she did succeed as an artist. He had never cared for art, but a lot of people did. People respected artists, especially the successful ones.

"I want you to be happy," he said, willing to let this play out and see where it went. She'd have the summer to dabble in her art, maybe gain a little recognition. He'd be there for her, support her efforts because he loved her and wanted her to be happy. But by fall she'd have a baby and their whole life would change...for the better.

ABOUT STELLA MACLEAN

Stella MacLean is the author of sixteen works of fiction and one of non-fiction. She has given workshops throughout North America, served on the board of Romance Writers of America, and was Writer in Residence at Vancouver Public Library in 2018. Young Love is her seventeenth work of fiction.

You can contact Stella by:

Website: www.stellamaclean.com
Twitter: @Stella_MacLean
Facebook: facebook.com/stella.maclean.3

www.ingramcontent.com/pod-product-compliance
Lightning Source LLC
Chambersburg PA
CBHW031345170626
46807CB00002B/833